THE SAINT OF MARS

"...this compact, swiftly paced story stays tense and bursts with scenes of desperate action."
—**PUBLISHERS WEEKLY**

"...this is genre-fiction gold."
—**BLUEINK REVIEW** (STARRED REVIEW)

"Another blistering installment with a cool, clever female lead."
—**KIRKUS REVIEWS** (STARRED REVIEW)

"A delightful slice of science fiction noir."
—**KEITH R.A. DECANDIDO,** AUTHOR OF *ALIEN: ISOLATION*

THE MINDS OF MARS

"Recommended for all fans of speculative mysteries."
—**PUBLISHERS WEEKLY**

"Denver Moon: The Minds of Mars combines Blade Runner and the original Total Recall with a dash of old-school detective noir that is hard to put down and leaves the reader wanting more." — **INDIEREADER**

"A searing mystery with a superlative, gun-toting protagonist."
—**KIRKUS REVIEWS** (STARRED REVIEW)

"This is cinematic science fiction, moving at a fast pace and building up a complex world."
—**CLARION REVIEWS**

"Readers looking for adrenaline-fueled and downright fun literary escapism should look no further than Denver Moon."
—**BLUEINK REVIEW** (STARRED REVIEW)

"*Denver Moon: The Minds of Mars* is noir sci-fi at its best. A powerful story that is hard to put down and highly recommended for mystery and sci-fi fans alike."
—**MIDWEST BOOK REVIEWS**

METAMORPHOSIS

"The skilled, perpetually poised detective shines brightly in this series, be it a novel, comic book, or any other format."
—**KIRKUS REVIEWS** (STARRED REVIEW)

DENVER MOON: THE THIRTEEN OF MARS

Copyedits by Bret Smith, Jeanni Smith, and Calvin Newland
Cover art by Aaron Lovett and Matt Hubel
Cover design by Joshua Viola
Denver Moon logo by James Viola
Interior art by Aaron Lovett
Typesets and formatting by Alec Ferrell

A HEX PUBLISHERS BOOK

Published & Distributed by Hex Publishers, LLC
PO BOX 298
Erie, CO 80516

www.HexPublishers.com

Print ISBN-13: 978-1-7365964-6-3
Ebook ISBN-13: 979-8-9862194-1-7

First Hex Edition: 2022

10 9 8 7 6 5 4 3 2 1

Printed in the U.S.A.

DENVER MOON

THE THIRTEEN OF MARS

WARREN HAMMOND & JOSHUA VIOLA

HEX PUBLISHERS

For Orion

CHAPTER ONE

MY GRANDFATHER STOPPED MARCHING, AND for a second, I thought something might be wrong, but I could hear his breathing through the speaker in my helmet. It sounded just the same as it had for the whole hike.

"C'mon," I said. "We're almost there. Then we can take a break." After a half hour of walking on the Martian surface, I was eager to get inside and out of my enviro-suit.

Ojiisan dropped to his knees. I rushed to him. "Are you okay?"

"Look at this rock," he said, no sign of distress in his voice. He was fine.

I put a relieved hand over my pounding heart. We'd become close these last two years. Sure, we carried a trainload of baggage between us, but other than some occasional sniping, we'd learned to keep it stowed away. Just like any family. "Don't scare me like that."

"Sorry," he said. "But do you see this?"

I knelt down next to him. Peering through my faceplate, I failed to see what had drawn his attention. It looked like a regular rock in the sand to me. One of millions littering this barren desert of a world. "What do you see?"

He pointed at the rock's face with a gloved finger. "Look at it. Isn't that amazing?"

I leaned closer and stared. "What am I looking at?"

"Can't you see it? It's right there."

Again, I tried to see whatever it was that caught his eye, but all I saw was craggy stone.

"It's a lichen," he said. "Here on Mars. A lichen."

"Wow," I said, though I still couldn't see it. "I guess the terraforming project has entered a new phase."

"Indeed, it has," he said. "You still can't see it, can you?"

"You know I'm colorblind."

"You got your monochromism from me, Denver," he said. "But I can see it clear as day. It's practically blanketing the side of the rock that faces the sun."

I tried one more time to see it, but it was invisible to me.

<What have I been telling you?> asked the voice in my mind. <You're going blind, Denver.>

<I can see well enough,> I said to Smith, the AI who lives in my gun and speaks directly into my head. <It's just the sandstorms. Everything's hazy today.>

<No, it's not. The atmospheric particulate count is the low-

est it's been in six weeks. It's your eyes. It's time to get them replaced.>

My grandfather was on the move again. Despite his age, he was practically racing down the hillside. "Look at it all," he called. "It's everywhere!"

I stood tall, my eyes scanning the area. Stretching toward the horizon was a rippling sea of dust and sand. At the bottom of the slope, I saw the black blur of oxygen generators. Behind them was a massive smear of solar collectors. I had to admit that making out the fine details was getting tougher every day, especially over the last couple years. But I wasn't blind. Not yet. I could see everything I needed to see.

Except for the lichens that were evidently all around me. But I wasn't going to worry over that. Despite never having seen a lichen in person, I'd seen pictures. They were just crusty little growths that clung to the surface. Barely more than a stain. What was the big deal if I couldn't see them?

"Can you believe it?" said Ojiisan. "Mars is alive!" His voice sounded happier than I'd ever heard it. I wondered if this was what he sounded like when he landed on Mars so many years ago, when he and the late Cole Hennessey founded the colony and started to erect Mars City. When Mars, *his* Mars, became humanity's last best hope after Earth had become a wasteland.

"Today it's lichen," he said. "Tomorrow, forests and pastures."

"We're a long way from that." Immediately, I regretted

putting voice to the thought. The fact that Mars could sustain life, even something as primitive as a lichen was a *huge* deal. It might be centuries before the planet was truly livable, but that shouldn't stop us from celebrating what was monumental progress. "Tomorrow feels closer than ever," I said with genuine excitement.

I trailed Ojiisan along the last few hundred feet of rough terrain to the research facility. I punched the keypad and the door lifted to allow entry into the airlock. Sitting down on the steel bench, we listened to the whir of air pumps and waited for the light to flash before popping the seals on our helmets and wriggling out of our suits.

"You ready for this?" asked Ojiisan.

I grinned and shook my head. "Am I ever ready to see Doctor Werner?"

"It's been almost two years since you've seen him face-to-face. I thought you'd be missing him by now."

From the airlock, we entered the main hallway. "You remember the way to his office?"

Ojiisan led us to the right and down a set of stairs. "Third lev down," he said. "That's where we'll find his living quarters."

He should have said *nest*. Doctor Stuart Werner was a bug. An alien who had spent years trying and failing to seize control of our minds. He wanted to enslave us, to reduce the whole of the human race to mindless worker bees. Drones who would serve him as our queen.

I wished we could have exterminated the bugs who

infiltrated Mars City, but the aliens had the ability to shapeshift, to walk among us as if they were human. Some were known to my grandfather and me as the bugs they were. Others remained undiscovered so they could spy and scheme and continue to work toward their goal of mental enslavement like they'd done so many times before to so many races across the galaxy.

I hated them. An ever-existing threat. The very thought of them filled me with dread that stuck in my throat like a stim pill. Every ounce of happiness I'd managed to squeeze from life these last two years was dampened and darkened by their presence. They were always there. And they were trying like mad to crack our brains. To strip us of everything we were and turn us into lobotomized zombie slaves. To lay their proverbial eggs in our gray matter.

I shivered. Couldn't help it. I'd seen quite a few of them in their natural form and every single one of them provoked the same nauseating unease. Some were spider-like with spindly legs and bodies covered by furry bristles. Others were more reminiscent of a centipede's long segmented body except their skin was shiny and oily as an eel.

Doctor Werner though, he was a cockroach. I'd never had the displeasure of seeing him in bug form, but when I pictured it, I always saw a cockroach. A dirty, disgusting roach who filled me with the urge to squish him under my heel.

But much as I wanted to, I couldn't. We needed him.

Without him, there wouldn't be a terraforming project, and without the terraforming project, humanity would find a way to perish soon enough.

As much as I detested the thought, Doctor Werner was our only hope. His kind was so much more technologically advanced than us. They understood biology at a level that was both incomprehensible and unimaginable to the best of our scientists. They were masters of the environment too. Tens of thousands of times before, they turned hunks of lifeless rock like Mars into thriving gardens full of bounty.

So we had no choice but to let Werner and the others stay here. As long as he was willing to make Mars habitable, we gave him all of the resources he requested. To keep him safe, we hid his true nature and identity from all but a select few humans. To keep him focused, we exiled him to the far side of the planet two years ago, where he could work all by himself commanding an army of machines and terraforming factories that spanned the entire planet.

In return, he and his kind kept trying to unlock the secrets of our brains so that two to three hundred years from now, when this planet became a new Eden, it could be theirs. The richest and most powerful of the aliens would come to settle this world that they would call their own, and it would be prepopulated with a workforce of slave labor.

That was their way.

And ours, I'd decided, was to never give up hope.

Despite their best efforts, the human brain had so far proven to be resistant to mind control. We were unique that way. After so many intelligent species had fallen into their mental stranglehold, we still stood free and fiercely independent. Plus, we had tech of our own. Though they were the undisputed masters of biology, ecology, geology, and most any other -ology, we were better at AI. Of all the species of the galaxy, we were the only ones who dared to create the botsies. We were the only people audacious enough to craft sentient beings inside our computer systems, like Smith, my best friend and confidant. How, exactly, that might give us the edge we needed to stay free, I didn't know. But it was something.

"Are you sure Werner won't mind me tagging along?" I asked.

"We'll find out soon enough," Ojiisan said.

I stopped. "What does that mean? He's not expecting me?"

Ojiisan turned and I caught a glimpse of a grin. "He's not expecting *us*. Best to keep him on his toes."

I sighed. "Great."

Ojiisan chuckled and continued down the stairs. "We'll be fine. I'm sure that pistol of yours is ready for any possible threat."

<Smith, you know what that means.>

<Way ahead of you, Denver. I've been in killmode since you walked through the front door.>

At the bottom of the stairway, I followed my grandfather to the left and into a room haphazardly lit by dozens of impossibly bright spotlights that randomly flicked on and off. I put up a hand to shade my squinting eyes. "Jesus, how can he stand it?"

"Lightning," said Ojiisan. "It's meant to simulate a massive lightning storm."

"How do you know that?"

"I asked him the last time I was here. His species is originally from a world so ravaged by lightning storms the planet itself is practically electrified."

"It's been ten seconds and I already have a headache."

<You need new eyes, Denver.>

<Gimme a break, Smith. It's like a million flashbulbs are going off in front of my face.>

<Your grandfather seems to be adjusting without issue.>

I looked at Ojiisan. He was squinting just as bad as I was. <Like hell he is.>

I stepped forward and my boot slipped out from under me. I reached for the wall to steady myself, but it was too late, and I fell backward to land spine-jarringly on my ass. I let out a groan and rubbed my jaw where my teeth had snapped together.

"Are you okay, Denver?" asked Ojiisan from the other side of the puddle. On the floor, right where I'd stepped, was a wide pool of goo. The boot print I'd left in the middle was a sloppy skid.

I looked for my grandfather's boot prints but there weren't any. Clearly, he'd seen the puddle and had the good sense to step over it.

<Told you so.>

I pressed myself upright, thankful that I hadn't landed in the slick ooze. Stepping around the puddle, I followed Ojiisan into the long cave of a room. As we went deeper, we found walls strangled by vines and pipes that dripped stringy glops.

It got hotter and hotter the farther we went. My stomach turned at the smell coming from the ventilation system that reminded me of the Mars City methane pits. I reached a hand for Smith and gripped the handle. "Was it like this the last time you were here?" I asked Ojiisan.

"Not at all. It looked just like his old lab in Mars City, but that was six months ago."

I slipped Smith from his holster and held him out front with two hands.

<Stand down, Denver. I just scanned the area. There's nobody here.>

I lowered him but kept a finger hovering over the trigger. "Smith says nobody's here."

"If Doctor Werner isn't here, where is he?" Ojiisan said.

Smith tapped a rack of servers to look for any electronic records that might offer some clues as to what happened here. I wiped sweat from my forehead, unsurprised to see that my shirt was already soaked. "I know you came out here six months ago, but when was the last time you talked to Werner?"

"Maybe two weeks ago," said Ojiisan.

"Video conference?"

He shook his head. "Audio only."

"So he could've been anywhere when you spoke to him. We need to track down the source of that call and find out where he went."

<On it, Denver.>

"Good," said Ojiisan. "Let me know what he says."

Though my grandfather and Smith shared no means of direct communication, he knew my AI well enough to know he was always listening through my ears. He also knew Smith well enough to assume he was already digging into the communication records. He and Smith shared a personality after all. They shared the same memories too, at least up until recent history.

"Let's search the rest of the building," said Ojiisan.

I nodded and followed him toward the door that led to the bio lab.

<The calls came from offplanet, Denver.>

"You're saying Doctor Werner left Mars?" I responded out loud so Ojiisan could follow my side of the conversation.

<For the last four months, all calls coming from the doctor came from an IP lease that hasn't been used in twenty years. He's been running the terraforming project remotely for months now.>

"Who was the IP address leased to?"

<A defunct oil company on Earth.>

"That can't be."

<It's true. Doctor Werner is on Earth, and he's managed to

get a communication station set up.>

"What is it?" asked Ojiisan. "You look like you just stepped on a nail."

CHAPTER TWO

I PUSHED THROUGH A SET OF DOUBLE DOORS. Rows and rows of scrubby foliage grew from vertical planters hanging from the walls. Succulents arranged on grated shelves baked beneath florescent tubes. Racks suspended from a tall ceiling stored thousands of Petri dishes that were arranged in piles like poker chips. Robotic arms swung from tracks that ran overhead. Moving with speedy precision, the arms used pincers to relocate one Petri dish at a time like they were vinyl in a vast biological jukebox. Water trickled into gutters on the floor, and grow lights were so hot on my skin, I thought—for the first time in my life—I should be wearing sunscreen.

"Amazing," said Ojiisan. "Someday soon the whole planet will be blanketed with growth."

I couldn't help but be awed by the scale of what was happening here. Climbing a step ladder, I was able to see a stack of Petri dishes where algae and molds sprouted.

Knowing that there were hundreds of facilities just like this one spread across Mars filled me with pride. We could *do* this. We could turn this dusty, lifeless rock into a beautiful paradise. Now, more than ever, I wished we had lifespans half as long as the bugs so I could survive to see it.

<I've gained access to the records,> said Smith. <It's mostly scientific data, but I've also found a cache of offworld communications.>

<What do they say?>

<I don't know. Only the message metadata is visible, so I know the communications came in right before Doctor Werner went to Earth, but I can't read any of the messages themselves. They're all encrypted.>

<Where did these messages come from?>

<They were relayed through Station Sixty-Six.>

Station Sixty-Six was in the belts. <Who would he be talking to out there?>

<I said the communication was *relayed* through Station Sixty-Six. It didn't originate there. Whoever he was talking to was somewhere in deep space.>

<So he's been talking to the bugs.>

<That's the reasonable assumption, yes.>

I'd known about the bugs for two and a half years now, but I still knew so little about them. I didn't know where they came from, or how many different types there were. I didn't know how their government worked or anything about their financial system. I didn't know a thing about their language or food sources or natural habitats.

All I knew was a few of them had come to conquer Mars, and Doctor Werner was their leader. At least he was their leader until he fled to Earth for reasons as mysterious as everything else that was bug-related.

"What do you think is in there?" asked Ojiisan. I hustled to catch up to where he stood before a large metal door that resembled a bank vault.

"One way to find out." I spun the hatch wheel until the locking mechanism clanked open.

Pulling hard, I felt a whoosh of cool air rush past when I broke the seal. We stepped into an unlit space. The floor felt spongy under my boots. Ojiisan pulled a penlight from his pocket and flicked it on. The beam stretched just a few feet before being swallowed by the darkness.

Shoulder-to-shoulder, we walked across a mossy blanket that gave off a peaty smell. Following the beam of my grandfather's penlight, I saw banks of drawers built into the walls. Choosing a button at random, I pushed it with my thumb. With a hiss, a drawer slid slowly open. White clouds of chilled gas poured over the drawer's lip and waterfalled to the floor. I waved the vapors away so we could see what was inside.

Marbles. That was what they looked like. Hundreds of them were piled into the drawer, each one perfectly round and glinting brightly inside the penlight's beam.

I reached for one. Expecting it to feel hard to the touch, I was surprised to find its surface gave slightly to the press of my fingertips. I held it close to the light, thinking I might be able to see into its glassy, gem-like interior.

<Denver?>

Ignoring the voice speaking into my mind, I continued to study the strange object. Returning it to the drawer, I picked up a different one twice the size of the first.

<Denver, I think you better put that down.>

Again, the light couldn't penetrate the opaque object. I squeezed it between my thumb and forefinger wondering if it might pop like a cherry tomato.

When I applied more pressure, it jumped out from between my fingers to fall back into the drawer like it was attached to an invisible string. I sucked in a breath. What the hell?

<I'm picking up life signs, Denver. Lots of them since you opened that vault.>

I heard something overhead. Ojiisan heard it too, his penlight now aimed straight up into the dark. It was a wet sound, similar to the one made by a plunger. The hair on the back of my neck stood up, and I grabbed hold of Ojiisan's elbow as I eased the two of us toward the door. More slurps sounded above, this time accompanied by a chorus of chittering clicks and clacks.

Stringy globs of a slime stretched down from the shadows. Molasses-like, the thick goop oozed all the way to the floor before puddling in front of the door.

Something jumped from the dark. The size of a piece

of fruit, it had a wobbly, amorphous shape as it lobbed itself in my direction. I jumped backward, avoiding the worst of the gooey splatter. I wasn't fast enough to dodge the second one, which struck my foot with a wet slap. Almost instantly, my foot was cemented in place, and the skin around my ankles began to burn where the substance had soaked through my sock.

Ojiisan stood on the other side of the giant metal door, ready to close it, but I couldn't join him until I freed my unbudgeable foot.

"Hurry, Denver!"

I reached down and yanked at my shoelaces, my fingertips rewarded by the same itchy burn that had sunk into my ankle. The laces came loose, and my foot slipped mercifully free. I hustled through the doorway an instant before my grandfather slammed it shut with a clang and spun the hatch wheel. He was already running when he said, "C'mon, let's get to the airlock."

There was nothing I wanted more than to get out of there, but my ankle felt like it had been stung by a hundred bees. I reached for my sock and quickly stripped it off before racing to catch up to Ojiisan. Jesus, my fingers were on fire now, too.

<Denver, my scans show the toxin on your ankle and hands is laced with formic acid. Don't wipe your eyes. Your vision's bad enough as it is.>

<No shit, Smith!>

I scrubbed my hands on my pants and as I ran, a loud clang sounded from behind me. Exiting Doctor Werner's lab, I stole a final look back to see if the vault was still closed. It wasn't.

Bugs, dozens of them, were tumbling through the doorway in a churning mass of pistoning legs and clacking jaws and claws.

Making it to the stairs, I followed Ojiisan up. His pace was slow as he struggled for breath. I put a hand on his back, careful not to touch any exposed skin, and urged him upward faster than either of us thought he could go. They were closing on us, the sound of their scrambling and skittering filled the stairwell. We exited the stairs and sprinted for the airlock. Ojiisan fell, and I dragged him the last few feet before slamming the door and spinning the hatch wheel.

I didn't wait for us to put on our enviro-suits before starting the air clearing cycle. I snatched my gear from its hook and stuck my stinging bare foot into the booted leg. The hatch wheel started to reverse, but Ojiisan managed to grab hold of it before it could complete a full revolution.

I checked to verify that the light over the door was on. "What are they doing? We'll lose containment if they open that door!"

Ojiisan didn't have enough breath in his lungs to respond. Instead, he looked for something he could use to jam the hatch shut, but there was nothing in the airlock. I went to him and zipped up his suit as far as I could, then grabbed the hatch wheel myself so he could finish the job on his own. There was tension on the wheel. I felt them trying to rotate it open, but it took barely any effort to hold the wheel steady. Score one for opposable thumbs.

Once his helmet was in place, Ojiisan took the wheel from me, and I continued to wriggle into my suit. It occurred to me then that they'd have an easier time turning that wheel if they took human form, but whatever those bugs were, they must not be the shapeshifting kind.

<Don't seal me inside the suit, Denver.>

I pulled Smith from my belt and set the gun on the bench until I finished zipping up. Helmet sealed, I nodded at Ojiisan who opened the outer airlock door, the sprawl of Martian desert right outside. I took Smith in my free hand and nodded at my grandfather to let go of the wheel. We ran outside and I reached for the lever that would drop the exterior door behind us, but the inner door burst open before I got the chance. A gust of wind from the pressurized facility hit me like a truck. Smith fell from my hands as I flew backward into the semi-vacuum of Martian atmosphere. I landed hard, my hip taking the worst of it. I flipped onto my stomach in time to see dozens of bugs rolling to a stop after being ejected by the rush of decompression.

<To your right, Denver. I'm to your right!>

Lifting myself onto all fours, I crawled toward the Smith & Wesson. I didn't expect the bugs to live long out here with no air, but they could live long enough to do plenty of damage. I grabbed hold of Smith. Time to unleash the pulseripper.

"Duck!" I yelled into my mouthpiece. My grandfather threw himself to the ground and I fired. A blast rippled outward, and a swath of bugs blew apart. Globs of goo flew every which way, but I kept my feet planted and squeezed the trigger again. I felt the sand crunch beneath me each time Smith unleashed a pulse. My grandfather scrambled to get behind me as I took out as many of them as I could. Gods, there must have been a couple hundred of them. I kept firing, the good news being they seemed to be slowing down as oxygen deprivation took its toll.

I spun around and picked off a few of the stragglers. By the time I came full circle, a bug had come within just a few feet of Ojiisan. I squeezed off a shot, but even with the help of Smith's targeting system, it went hopelessly wide.

The bug leapt at my grandfather. He put up his hands but couldn't ward it off. He and the bug went down in a dusty tumble of spindly legs and snapping pincers. I charged ahead to Ojiisan and slammed the butt of the pistol into the bug's head. The creature's shell gave way and Smith sank into sticky, tar-like gunk.

The bug went still. Yanking Smith out of the wound, I fired three more times to finish off the last of those who were still moving.

<I can't see anything, Denver. My sensors are covered in bug guts.>

<Now who's the blind one?>

"How's your air supply?" asked Ojiisan.

"Slim," I said. "I would've changed tanks if we had the chance. I'll be running on fumes for the last leg of the hike, but I can make it. You?"

"I'm good." He lifted himself upright. "We can't go back inside. There will be more."

The whole area was littered with death. "Maybe we got them all."

"You saw those drawers. They were full of eggs, thousands and thousands of them."

Eggs? Was that what those things were? I remembered how one jumped from my fingers, and a shiver shimmied up my spine. "Oh hell," I said.

"They didn't shapeshift. Based on the way they sacrificed themselves to the atmosphere, I doubt they had much intelligence."

"Like soldier ants."

"Yes."

We started walking. It was a long way back to the fuel station where we'd left the shuttle.

Eggs. So many of them. And this was just one facility. There were hundreds of others around Mars, and I didn't need to check them to know that they had all been filled with nurseries. Somehow, Werner managed to shield those nurseries from scans that might've indicated the tens of thousands of life signs.

"The doctor must've grown tired trying to crack our minds," said Ojiisan.

"Right," I said. "Now his plan is extermination."

CHAPTER THREE

MY LUNGS WERE FEELING IT NOW. THE pressing, aching, pain of oxygen starvation. But the fuel pad was visible. Another five minutes, and we'd be inside our shuttle.

"We have to call the Peerless Leader," I said between breaths.

The Church of Mars was the most powerful institution this world had to offer. Its influence practically doubled in the last two years as it moderated many of its positions. This was all since the church's founder, Cole Hennessey, had been martyred for everyone to see. The church's hard-liners still ran the show, but their kinder, friendlier image makeover had swelled the pews.

The government, on the other hand, had very few resources. Mars had no military, and the planet's security forces were corrupt to the point of being useless to the average citizen. So it was the church who stood the best chance of mobilizing against the invasion.

"Those facilities have to be destroyed." I couldn't help but cringe as I said it. The only thing that united Martians was our hope that one day the terraforming project would succeed, and our children's children wouldn't live like rats in the maze of tunnels we called Mars City. Destroying the terraforming facilities would set back the project by decades if not centuries. But what else could we do?

"You're awfully quiet," I said. "Are you okay?" I stopped and turned around. Ojiisan wasn't there. My heart leapt into a new gear. "Ojiisan?"

Back over the rise, I saw a puff of sand that quickly evaporated, and I ran for it. After spotting a second poof of Martian dust, I picked up my pace, but my muscles were sluggish and slow and my burning lungs sapped what little energy I had. "Ojiisan?"

"I can't—" His voice was weak, and I cranked my speakers to max volume. "I can't go any farther," he said.

Cresting the hill, I could see him now. He took one more shuffle, kicking up a cloud of dust in the process, and sat down. Fueled by panic, I hurried as fast as I could. A light on his air tank winked in and out.

"What happened?" I shouted. "You said you had enough air!"

"Punctures in my suit," he wheezed. "The hair on those bugs is sharp."

"Goddammit, we could've patched the punctures."

"There are too many holes."

I reached him and pulled emergency patch tape from

the pocket of my leg. "Where are the holes?"

"You don't have time for this," he said. "Your air is low too."

"Is that why you didn't tell me?"

"I should've let you go alone after the attack. But I wanted to be with you a little longer, Magomusume."

I grabbed him and moved my faceplate close. "Where are the holes?"

"Everywhere. You can't fix them all."

I clutched at his suit, searching for rips and tears, but wherever the punctures were, they were too small for my eyes see. I unzipped my suit and yanked at the tube that ran to my emergency water supply. I aimed the hose at one of the scuffed areas of his garb and squeezed the bladder dry of two pints before zipping back up. I studied the wet area of his suit closely, looking for telltale air bubbles to show me where the holes were, but all I could see was a hazy blur of polymer fabric. Damn these eyes!

"Go," he said before his eyelids closed. "Mars is yours now."

CHAPTER FOUR

I DRAGGED OJIISAN THROUGH THE CARGO DOOR, cycled the airlock, and popped his helmet before mine. Sweet air whooshed in and I sucked deep, wheezing breaths. I patted his face. "C'mon, we're inside now. You can breathe."

I yanked off my gloves. My fingertips were dry now, but they were covered with painful splotchy burns from that bug goop on my shoelaces. I didn't want to see my ankle, but I was thankful the chafing pain I felt with every step probably kept me from passing out as I dragged Ojiisan the rest of the way here. I pressed my fingers against his neck but my numb fingertips couldn't feel anything.

"Ojiisan, I need to you wake up, understand?"

I held my hand near his nose to see if I could feel his breath. The faintest whisper of air gave one of my burns a slight sting. My eyes welled and tears spilled onto my cheeks. "Stupid old man," I said. With the back of my hand, I wiped my cheeks before patting his again. "Wake up now. You're safe."

But he didn't wake up. He didn't move at all. I used a knuckle to push one of his eyelids open only to have it shut again. I pinched his arm. Nothing. I pinched it again, this time using all the force my fingers could muster. Still nothing.

<Denver, clean me off so I can take a look.>

I scrubbed the bug gunk from one of Smith's sensors with my shirt and pointed him at Ojiisan.

<What do you see? How are his vitals?>

The voice in my head was silent.

<Smith! What do your scans show?>

<His vitals... I—I'm sorry, Denver...>

I sat across from the specialist as she said things like *coma* and *lack of brain activity*. She spoke these things like she was reading items off a shopping list. There was no compassion. Two days of poking and prodding my grandfather and she couldn't even find the time to sit in front of a mirror and practice some basic goddamn human emotion. Smith emoted better than she did. There was no attempt to soften any one of the blows that hit me like the repeated waves of a tsunami. *Unrecoverable brain damage. Vegetative.*

I sat silent. More than anything, I wanted to anesthetize myself. I wanted to zone out on neuroin. Like the good ol' days, I wanted to hit it so hard I wouldn't feel a thing for a month. A year. Cocooned in a haze, I'd be impervious to this onslaught. *Feeding tube. End-of-life directives.*

I tried to bottle up the anguish that made it difficult to breathe, the sob-inducing pain that made my gut seize, the rage that made me want to flip the specialist's desk.

She asked me a question. I could hear it in the way her voice raised pitch. Could see it in the way she leaned forward in her chair, her eyes expectant. But I wasn't listening anymore.

She repeated it, but I didn't care what she wanted to know. "Discharge him," I said. "He's coming with me."

Her eyes pinched, and she did a double take. "Excuse me?"

"Check him out of the hospital."

"I can't do that. He's immobile. Anybody in his state requires around-the-clock care."

"I'm taking him with me."

"Taking him where? Home?"

No. Not home. But I left that particular thought unsaid. "Nanobots can keep him alive, correct?"

"They can't restore brain function."

"But they can keep his organs going?"

"Yes, they can keep his body functioning, but the grandfather you knew won't be coming back. He went without oxygen for twenty minutes."

"That's not true. I connected his air supply to mine

once every minute during that twenty minutes I dragged him."

She sighed. "That was heroic, but you told me yourself you only gave him a ten second count each time, and your air supply was weak, and what little air he got quickly dissipated because his suit was leaking. I'm sorry, Denver. I know you did your best, but his brain still starved."

"How long will it take to prepare the nanobots?"

"I don't know. Maybe a day. But that's not happening."

"Yes, it is." I stood. "You have twenty-four hours to get him ready and then I'm taking him with me."

I hurried out of her office, down the hall, and stopped at his room to stand in the doorway. Electronic pings sounded with cold mechanical precision that created a dark melody along with the whoosh of his ventilator. His skin was ashen, his face still. We'd lost so many years when he was exiled to the southern desert. Then when he came back to me, we lost many more months due to my petty unwillingness to forgive. But these last two years were special. I wasn't ready to be an orphan again.

I'd saved him once. I could save him again.

I turned and made for the closest exit. More than anything, I needed fresh air, as if such a thing were possible on Mars. Glass doors whisked open and I stepped from one tunnel into another, but at least this one—though crowded—wasn't as cramped.

The air tasted gritty. Sandstorms had abated quite a bit in the last year or two, but a rager currently swirled above Mars City, and even here, twelve levs deep into Mars's crust, the dust still managed to worm through vents and filters to coat all surfaces with a film that required constant wipe-downs. I considered taking Ojiisan uplev. They had the best care facilities on Mars there. But there was no way they'd keep quiet about Mars City's only living co-founder being braindead. That had to stay under the radar until I found a way to get him fixed.

I sat on an empty bench. Twenty-four hours. I'd set myself a helluva short deadline. I had so much to do before then, but right now, I needed to sit and gather my thoughts. The last two days were split between the healing ward and meetings with the Peerless Leader. She already sent raiding parties to two of the terraforming facilities. The first was a successful eradication effort. The second failed, and eleven people plus two botsies died. She needed to recruit a much stronger force which meant finally telling the public their suspicions were true. There were aliens among us, and they plan to exterminate us.

Much as I wanted to join the eradication forces, Ojiisan was my first priority. He was Mars. The man who, along with the deceased Cole Hennessey, built Mars City. On this world, he was unique in stature and respect. A unifier. Mars needed him.

I needed him.

I also needed Navya. Nigel too if he could be pried away from his latest project. But first, I had to steal a little more time for myself. I had one more decision to make, and if I was going to do it, I'd have to do it now.

I looked at the tunnel stretched before me. Twenty feet wide, its fifty-foot walls were composed of tall panes of glass. Enclosed behind the glass was an array of hexagonal storefronts stacked like honeycomb. Neon signs blinked and hummed. *Cut-rate Cut Shop. Cancer-B-Gone. Triple-X Body Enhancement.*

I shivered and felt fortunate I had the funds to get my grandfather better care than any of these hacks and charlatans who preyed on those who couldn't afford Mars's only reputable healing ward downlev. Still, I stared at one particular sign, barely legible with my blurry monochrome vision.

I told myself to get going, but my feet stayed planted right where they were. I'd been resisting this idea for so long it was hard to commit even though the decision was already made.

Eager for distraction, I let a ruckus in the alleyway draw my gaze. An old woman zipping along in a motorized hoverchair forced the crowd to part. Hawkers still bombarded her with holographic before-and-after images of weight loss and youth restored. She sped right through them. The healing ward doors swished open for her, but then she spotted me right before entering and hit the brakes so hard I thought she'd be ejected from her chair.

"You," she said. "It's you...I'm about to get test results. Bless me, will you?"

"Leave me alone," I told her. I might've been sainted by the church, but I was just a regular person. I had no divine powers that could help this woman's ailments.

She stayed where she was, her brow scrunched up like she hadn't understood me. "Git," I said, "or I'll shove you through those doors myself."

My grandfather was braindead and Mars was about to be overrun by bugs heralding the extinction of the human race, and this woman wanted me to blow hocus pocus up her wrinkled ass?

The old bat let out a heavy sigh of indignation but finally did as she was told. I knew my grandfather would disapprove. He was always telling me to be gracious. Giving people like her a kind word or two cost so little of me that there was no reason I shouldn't do it, especially when it meant so much to them.

But my blessings only meant something to the easily-influenced livestock of this red rock. The church took advantage of their weak minds and manipulated them. That wasn't my job. I might be their heralded Saint of Mars, but the title was the only thing saintly about me.

I stood and located the neon sign again. The words blinked brightly from behind a group of robotic mannikins. *If You Can Dream It.*

CHAPTER FIVE

S HE TOOK THE EYEBALL FROM ITS DISH AND SET it on my shoulder before stepping back to take a look at me. "I like the golden iris for you. Striking, don't you think?"

It was all I could do to keep from shrugging the wet glob to the floor.

"Or we could go with something more traditional, if you prefer."

The skin of her face was tighter than vacuum sealed plastic, but her bony hands were liver-spotted with age. The name *Cassidy* blinked in and out of static from an outdated holographic name badge fastened to her lapel. She wore the requisite lab coat, its thinning fibers failing to conceal the vibrant brassiere underneath. Her sleeves were too short to fully hide the faded tattoos of Burmese pythons branded with serial numbers that wrapped her forearms. With shaky fingers, she removed the eyeball from my shoulder and roughly dropped it into its dish before sealing it up and putting it back into the glass-doored refrigerator on a shelf labeled with a hand-written card that said *eyes*.

I brushed at the cold spot on my shoulder and immediately regretted it when my fingers came away damp. "I don't care much about the color," I said.

"You want to see better. I understand that. I'm surprised you didn't come to see me years ago. A bat's vision would test better than yours just did."

"That's a myth. Bats can see. Or at least they could before they went extinct."

"I was referring to a baseball bat." Cassidy laughed and gave the desk a slap. Despite my weak vision, I could see a lipstick stain on her teeth.

<Gods, Denver. You can't let her touch you.>

With no encouragement from me, she chuckled a few seconds more. "Okay, if you don't care about the color, then what do you care about?"

"I'm most interested in upgrades. Special abilities."

She grabbed a catalog from a drawer and put it on the desk. "We can order anything you like, night vision, zoom, infrared. These all come with recording devices. That's standard issue."

"How long does it take?"

"A week."

"They don't have eyes in stock?"

"Eyes don't last forever. They're made to order."

"I can't wait that long."

She put the catalog away. "I have another option.

Why don't you come back to my lab?"

<I really don't think this is a good idea, Denver.>

I followed her. <You've been after me for years to get my eyes replaced.>

<Replaced responsibly, by a reputable doctor.>

< You saw the diploma on the wall.>

<That was for massage therapy, Denver. She has no business touching a scalpel.>

Passing through a set of plastic flaps, we entered a chilled room that hummed with the sound of refrigerators, freezers and centrifuges. I followed into a long hallway where digital body-modeling software churned out dozens of naked holograms that blinked in and out of existence like a bizarre plastic surgery-themed hall of mirrors.

Next, we entered the operating room. A steel table stood in the corner. Below it sat a pair of plastic buckets that were so badly stained my stomach did a sickening flip. Above the table was a tangle of articulated arms tipped by the most godawful array of drills, lasers, and blades.

<You can't do this, Denver. That thing looks like a chandelier designed by Rafe.>

"Come, take a seat over here," she said.

Making sure not to touch the arms with my hands, I sat in an upholstered chair by the table. <I don't have a choice, Smith.>

<Of course, you do. Let's go back to the healing ward and see if we can get a walk-in appointment with somebody who

knows what they're doing.>

Cassidy was on her knees now, working at the lock to one of her fridges.

<There's no time,> I said. <I need this done now. We're leaving tomorrow.>

<Leaving where?>

Cassidy sat on a stool, a plastic box in her hands. "I'm going to show you something very special," she said. "Most people wouldn't believe what I'm about to tell you, but I don't want you to dismiss it so quickly."

She opened the box to reveal a pair of eyeballs. "These," she said, "are alien."

<Smith, is she telling the truth?>

<Scans indicate they most definitely aren't human...>

"Where did you get them?" I asked.

"I have a source. They walk among us, you know."

"I know."

Her eyes widened in surprise that I wasn't pushing back on her statement. Aliens were for cranks and conspiracy theorists. Little did she know that in another few hours, everybody would learn once and for all that they did indeed exist. A battle was on the horizon.

"They look like us," she said. "But they're not us. These eyes were manufactured in their lab. A patriot smuggled them out and brought them to me."

"For a fee."

"He got a nice payday indeed. But they do have a limited shelf life, so I'll give you a deal if you're interested."

"I told you I wanted special abilities. I want to see better than good."

"They're of alien manufacture," she said as if that was all the special I needed to hear.

"What can they do?"

She grinned. "There's only one way to find out."

<You can't be considering this, Denver.>

<Quiet.>

"Let me get my release forms and pricing sheets. If you commit right now, I'll have you seeing better by the end of the day."

<We have to get out of here,> said Smith. <I'll get you scheduled to see a real doctor.>

<No. It can't wait.>

<You've waited this long.>

<Dammit, that's exactly the problem. I couldn't see the holes, Smith.>

<What holes?>

I didn't respond. He'd figure it out soon enough.

<In your grandfather's suit? Those were just pinholes. Even a pair of good eyes might not have seen them. What happened to him wasn't your fault.>

Cassidy was back. I wiped a tear from my cheek. "Where do I sign?"

CHAPTER SIX

I LAY ON THE TABLE WHILE CASSIDY MADE preparations. "How much time do we have?" I asked. "I need to make a call."

"You've got five minutes," she said.

<Get Navya for me,> I told Smith.

<Do you want to speak through me or out loud?>

<Let's keep this private.>

A moment later, Navya's voice spoke directly into my head. <I was about to call you. Is what they're saying about a war true?>

<Yes, it's true, and it's going to be ugly,> I said, Smith matching my vocal patterns so closely Navya had no idea it was an AI relay coming from my mind.

<Holy shit. I don't know what you did this time, Den, but you went from rocking the boat to sinking it. Most aren't buying it, though. They're calling it another conspiracy.>

<That's probably for the best right now.>

<No doubt. I don't think the softies uplev could handle news

of aliens fucking with our heads. So, what's the plan?>

<I'm going offworld.>

<Running away? That's a first.>

<I wouldn't call it that.>

<Then what? Where are you going?>

<Earth.>

She was silent for a long time. When she finally spoke, she said, <Jesus, Denver. We're about to go to war with the bugs and you pick the one place that's even more dangerous.>

<I need a pilot, Navya.>

She took a deep breath. <I'll need a few hours to get my shit together. Should probably update my will while I'm at it.>

<That shuttle of yours is too small for a journey like this, though. See if you can get us something bigger before people realize this is real and start jumping ship. I'll pay for it. I'll pay your regular rates too.>

<Damn right you will. And hazard rates. So, why Earth?>

<Doctor Werner is there. We're bringing Ojiisan to him.>

<Denver... I know how much he meant to you, but—>

<*Means*, Navya. He *means* a lot to me. That's why we're going to Earth to save him.>

<You really think Doctor Werner can fix him?>

<He restored his memories once. He can do it again.>

<This time is different, Denver. He's brainde—> She stopped herself. <You understand that his brain doesn't work anymore, don't you?>

<It's all I have, Navya.>

I heard a sigh. I'd known her long enough to recognize it as a sign that she was about to drop the argument.

We'd been friends since we were kids, and the dynamic never changed. She was the giver, and I was the taker. I didn't know how to be anything else.

<I understand,> she said. <What the hell are we going to do locked up together for six weeks each way?>

<It'll be like when were roommates at the academy. We can watch old Earth movies.>

<Orphans unite.> I could picture the silly salute she just made.

A hot pain entered my arm. I turned in time to see Cassidy pull out a syringe. "Nighty-night."

"Damn, you could've warned me…"

She started pushing buttons on the anesthesia system.

<Navya, I gotta go.>

<What time tomorrow?>

<I don't know yet. I'll call.>

<I'll get things in order. Talk to you then.>

<Wait, Navya?>

<I'm here.>

<Make sure the ship has a recharging pod.>

<Is Nigel coming too?>

<He doesn't know it yet, but I'll find a way to talk him into it.> Cassidy lifted a mask to my face. <Talk to you soon, Navya, and thanks.>

Feeling woozy from the drugs in my bloodstream, I lifted my head just long enough for Cassidy to slip the mask over my head.

<There's still time to cancel this,> said Smith.

<No, th-there's n—>

I tried to open my eyes, but they were bandaged shut. My entire head ached like it did the last time I saw Rafe Ranchard. I heard footsteps nearby. "Hello?"

"Ah, you're awake," said Cassidy. "The bandages stay in place for twenty-four hours. Not a minute less, understand?"

I nodded.

"Then eyedrops every four hours for three days."

"Got it."

"You call me after you get those bandages off. Let me know what those eyes can do besides help you see straight. You never know when I might find another pair."

I stood to leave.

"You aren't going to get very far with those bandages on."

"My AI can guide me."

I took a step and kicked something in front of me that clattered to the ground. Cassidy chuckled.

"I have a better idea," she said. "There's a self-piloted hoverchair in the back you can borrow."

<I'd take her up on that, Denver,> Smith said.

I sighed. "Alright."

"I'll just need to input your address. Where's home?"

"I'm not going home," I said.

"It'll take you to wherever you wanna go."

"Red Tunnel. Jard Calder's place."

"Jard's? You go there too? His botsies are high-class. He sure knows how to program them to woo a lady, am I right?"

"Just put in the address and get me out of here."

"What's with the bandages, Denver? Did somebody finally get sick of your shit and pop you in the face?" said a gruff voice I instantly recognized as Jard's.

"Something like that," I muttered. "I need to talk to Nigel."

"He's in the workshop as usual," Jard said before blowing a thick cloud of something strong in my face. The aromas of vanilla and whipped cream meant he was puffing top shelf stuff. And if I knew Jard, it was laced with some sort of narcotic.

"Smells expensive," I said, waving a hand to fan the smoke away.

"You've got that right. Unicorn Milk. They're saying the world's about to go down the shitter. Might as well make the best of it."

"Mars has been in the shitter for a while now, Jard. So, about Nigel."

"Like I said, he's in the workshop."

I motioned to the bandages wrapped around my head. "I'll need an escort."

"I thought you'd never ask. Male or female? Maybe one of each to get you off? A combo? An old friend like you, I'll give you a freebie."

I chuckled and shook my head.

"Come," he said as he locked elbows with me. "Let's go find Nigel."

The botstringer led me to the workshop. Nigel had been leasing the space for the last year. To those on the outside, Jard was just a pimp. But he was also a talented engineer who knew more about botsie tech than anybody on Mars. When Nigel decided to create a new communication system for his kind, it only made sense to work out of Jard's workshop where he'd have access to top-of-the-line equipment and a mentor with the utmost abilities.

A door swished open and Jard guided me through before leaving.

"Bloody hell, what happened to you?" asked Nigel with his familiar English accent.

He took me into a hug before I had a chance to respond. His grasp was strong and befitting of the big brother I never had. "Finally decided to get rid of those eyes, did you? I was wondering when you'd get sick enough of that rubbish to do something about it." He released me. "What brings you here? I imagine it has to do with the news. Is it really war?"

"It sure seems that way."

"Bloody hell! What chance do we have?"

"Long term? Little to none. But the bugs in the nurseries we discovered in the terraforming facilities are still just eggs. That, and I don't think they have a means to attack the city right away. I didn't see any vehicles or aerial craft capable of moving a large force."

"We should just nuke the sites from orbit."

"And take out the Jericho project? You might not need oxygen to survive, Nigel, but, you know, we do."

He chuckled softly. "I suppose so. Does that mean you're planning to join the fight? Is that why you upgraded your eyes?"

"Actually, I was planning to take Ojiisan to Earth. I'm leaving tonight."

"Pray tell?"

"Doctor Werner is there."

"On Earth? Why?"

"I don't know. That's part of why I have to go."

"And the other part is you want to see if he can bring your grandfather's mind back?"

"Smith still carries his memories. It's worth a shot."

"Tatsuo isn't too far gone?"

I pinched my lips, frustrated that I kept getting asked the same question. It could be everybody else was right. My grandfather was gone and nothing would ever bring him back. But I wouldn't indulge such defeatism. When a shark stops swimming it dies, and I was a shark. My whole life I could only see one way to go, and that was forward at frenzied speed. The troubles—a shameful trail of addictions and failed relationships—came during the down periods. Better to always keep moving.

"So, why are you here, Denver?" asked Nigel.

"We were a good team. When you worked for me, the business never ran better."

"That we were. But I have work to do here. I might have made a breakthrough last week, and I need to monitor the testing I've instituted. How long does a round-trip to Earth take?"

"We'd be gone three months. Maybe longer."

Though I couldn't see him, I could picture him biting his lip like he always did when presented with a puzzle, a clever piece of programming to make him appear more human.

<Tell him he can bring his work, Denver,> Smith said. <You can delay departure by a few hours if you have to so he can bring what he needs.>

<Now you want to help? I thought you were against all of this.>

<I was against you getting your eyes scooped out by a quack. But Ojiisan needs us. We have to do what we can to bring him back, and we could use the extra muscle.>

<Good. Glad you see this my way.>

"You can bring your work, Nigel. We'll have plenty of time on the ship with nothing else to do."

<There,> I said to Smith. <I told him.>

<Tell him we *need* him. Tell him.>

<Will you cool it? Give him a minute to think it over. What's gotten into you all of a sudden?>

He didn't respond right away. I knew it was a sign he was about to say something I didn't want to hear. <Did it

ever occur to you to ask how I was doing?>

   <What are you talking about, Smith?>

   <I loved him too, you know.>

I could feel the blood drain from my cheeks. Gods, I wanted to crawl into a hole. It hadn't even occurred to me that Smith might be suffering too. For years, he struggled with his sense of self. He had Ojiisan's memories installed inside him, but I'd done more than that before he was ever brought online. I'd given him Ojiisan's personality, too. But the personality never quite fit right on Smith, and he'd been having bouts of an identity crisis ever since.

No, not ever since. His issues stopped when Ojiisan came back into our lives two years ago.

   <Regular contact with your grandfather made me feel much more grounded,> Smith said. <I felt like I knew what I was supposed to be when we were around him.>

As always in times of crisis, I'd been thinking exclusively of myself. It was so goddamned predictable. <I'm sorry, Smith. I've been selfish. We'll talk after liftoff, okay? I promise.>

"I'd have to bring a lot of equipment," said Nigel.

"Bring it," I said. "Whatever we have room for, bring it along."

"I'll have to make backups of several data stores. That could take a few hours."

"Take all the time you need. We'll wait."

CHAPTER SEVEN

OJIISAN AND I SAT IN AUTOMATED HOVER-chairs synced to Navya and Nigel who led us across a tarmac. I couldn't wait to get the bandages off my eyes but that wasn't supposed to happen for another six hours. In the meantime, the burden fell on Navya and Nigel to load the ship, an S-Class supply craft whose heyday had long since passed. According to Navya, the S-Class had the ability to land upon any terrain, and it came with plenty of space in its crew quarters. Provisions were already aboard as was a recharging pod that could keep Nigel operational.

The last bit of cargo was my grandfather, who was now breathing without a ventilator thanks to the nanobots residing near his brainstem. Tapped directly into his spine, they sent the signals necessary to keep his breathing muscles contracting and relaxing.

I thought I heard a siren. It was barely audible in the distance. "Do you hear that?"

Navya was first to respond. "Sounds like the old sand-storm warnings. Must be a storm outside."

Another siren sounded, this one close enough to make me wince at the ear-piercing wail. Navya and Nigel must've picked up the pace, my hoverchair now rattling across the bumpy airstrip. "What's happening? Can you see anything?"

I felt the concussion before I heard the explosion that tossed me to the ground. The ringing in my ears echoed loud enough to blot out even Smith's voice. I took a deep breath and covered my head as rubble pelted my body. Dirt and dust filled my mouth as shouts sounded all around me. I thought I heard Navya moaning and I crawled toward her whimpers. "Navya? Are you okay? Nigel?"

Another explosion erupted nearby. The ground vibrated under me, and I covered my head again. A rock struck my hip, a sharp pain shooting down my leg. Somebody grabbed my arm. "We're under attack," said Nigel. "Navya's hurt. I've got to get her and Tatsuo to the ship. I'll be back for you."

I nodded my understanding.

<The ship is close,> said Smith. <Keep your head down until he gets back.>

A scream sounded nearby.

<What's going on?>

<It's the bugs. They must have tunneled their way here. They blew holes in the ground and now they're pouring through from underneath.>

<How close are they?>

<Close.>

My already panicked heart kicked into another gear. <No time to stay down, Smith. We've gotta move. Now.>

<I can try to guide you, but it'll be dangerous, Denver. Keep your wits about you.>

I grabbed at the bandages over my eyes and ripped the tape free. I was immediately overwhelmed by a stabbing bright light. <Which way?>

<Behind you.>

I spun and stumbled forward, feet tripping on stones I couldn't see. The bugs were close enough that I could hear the clicking of their legs. I ran a few steps before tumbling back down. I couldn't see straight; my world was a hazy blur.

Something was on me. I could feel its hooks in my thigh. I swatted and rolled, but it only dug deeper into my flesh. I grabbed Smith and he fired a pulse. My hand was splashed with a wet, gooey blowback.

<Move, Denver! There's a swarm closing in behind you.>

<I can't see, Smith!>

<Brace yourself.>

<For what?>

I felt a familiar cold sting in my right palm as Smith injected me with stims. My heart raced as the drug pulsed through my veins. I scrambled upright and took off sprinting, hoping against all hope that I was running in the right direction. My vision started to sharpen, but all I could see was myself. It was me running with a blood-soaked pantleg. I stopped, blinked and shook my head, but I was still somehow looking at myself. But not just me, I could see a thousand of me. What the hell?

A bug latched onto my ankle, but the stims were doing their job now, numbing what would have been a painful bite. I looked down but couldn't see anything but a dizzying kaleidoscope of twisting, turning, colors.

Color!

For the first time in my life, my eyes were processing pigments—rusty reds, radiant yellows, warm oranges—on their own, without Smith tapping into my mind to trick my senses into believing I was seeing the real thing. I would have been mesmerized by the sheer beauty of it all if it wasn't for the creature gnawing on my foot. I pointed my Smith & Wesson and fired, trusting Smith's targeting system to do the job. The bug popped like a neon green pimple. I jerked my head in the direction of approaching clicks and clacks, but I moved too fast. My world spun and jerked and flipped upside-down. A wave of nausea cramped in my gut. I closed my eyes, but it didn't help, and I lost my balance, falling to the ground once more.

A bug clamped onto my right wrist and Smith fell from my spasming fingers. Another took a chunk out of my calf. With my left hand, I fished for Smith, but couldn't land upon him. My vision fractured into ten thousand discrete displays then coalesced into one fuzzy and unfocused smear.

With a painful rip, I tore the bug from my wrist but

more latched on with barbed legs that dug into me like hooks. Clacking mandibles chewed my flesh in a dozen places. I flailed my arms and legs to no avail.

I was moving, my thrashing form dragging across the tarmac.

<Smith!>

I heard Smith fire from his place on the ground, hitting some in the swarm as they splattered hot against my cheek.

<There's too many, Denver. I can't get them all.>

Were they taking me back to their nest? A little snack for their queen?

Something grabbed my arm with more pressure, tugging hard in the other direction. A bigger bug, probably. Maybe the swarm's leader.

"Cheeky buggers," Nigel said, pulling me from the melee.

He quickly swatted the bugs away, each one bringing a fresh round of agony as it ripped free before Nigel yanked me up the ramp and into the ship. "GO!" he shouted. I heard the hydraulics pull the ramp up.

"Smith?"

"Got him," Nigel said. "All five of us are aboard. You're leaking like a sieve. Let's get you patched up."

CHAPTER EIGHT

I SAT NEXT TO NAVYA ON THE BRIDGE. THE SKIN around her eyes had turned a deep shade of purple. She'd hit her head hard when knocked down by the first explosion.

Nigel patched up my bug bites as best as he could with what we had on the ship. None of them were too serious, and the vape-rock I huffed really took the edge off. I could see just fine now, still awestruck by the various tints and hues surrounding me. A long sleep had done wonders. Whatever I'd experienced when I first took those bandages off had to be chalked up to opening my eyes hours before the doctor said to do so. But if the doctor was to be believed, these eyes came from an alien lab. Who knew what they were trying to do? Whatever it was, it made me queasy.

Navya sipped her coffee, watching Mars slowly shrink out of sight. "I hope it's still there when we get back."

"Me too," I said. "We shouldn't be surprised the

aliens attacked the spaceport. The raids we've launched on the nurseries in the terraforming facilities all originated from there. If they can disable it, they might buy the time they need to hatch their army."

"How long will that take?"

I scratched at the regen bracelet around my ankle. It itched like hell. "Who knows? We still don't know much about them. What we do know is these bugs are different. They're not smart like the ones who shapeshift. These are like soldier ants. They just do what they're told."

"There was more than one species," she said. "Smith shared some of the footage he recorded while you were still sleeping. We counted at least a dozen different varieties."

"The bugs have conquered a lot of worlds. They probably have tens of thousands of different species in their hive. Their mind control systems are powerful."

"But they don't work on us," said Navya with more than a little pride.

"No, we won't become their drones. But that makes us their prey."

"Tell me about your progress," I asked.

Nigel looked up from his workstation and crossed his arms. "Denver, we need to talk."

I sighed. "It was insensitive of me not to ask about

your work. I get tunnel vision sometimes. All I could think about was getting this mission started. In the end, though, it's probably best I was in such a rush or we might not have launched at all. Don't you think so?"

"I understand how you are," he said. His tone wasn't angry or hurt. He stated it like it was simply a fact, which was why it cut so deep. "But that's not what I want to talk about."

"I know, I know," I said. "Just this once I promise to not make it about me, even though I kind of already did." I forced a smile. "Tell me about your work. Really, I want to hear about it."

"You keep misunderstanding me," he said. "I need to talk to you about something other than my work."

"We have six weeks for that. Give me an update on your progress first."

He shook his head in that what-can-you-do way, and I realized that in my desire to show how much I cared about his project, I just railroaded him again by controlling the topic of the conversation. I opened my mouth to tell him we could talk about whatever he wanted, but I closed it back up because he was already calling up holographic diagrams. For a change, maybe it was best to keep my mouth shut.

Nigel used his hand to spin a 3D schematic and pointed to one particular spot. "This is where I was stuck, but I was thinking about it all wrong."

I listened carefully though I could only understand a small percentage of what he was saying. For the last year, Nigel had been working on a communication system for botsies, but it wasn't based around the spoken word. He called it a much more *elemental* link in which language was unnecessary. He wanted to make it possible for botsies to transmit actual thoughts and emotion. I had no idea how such a thing was possible, but botsies were different from us humans. Humans were the result of an evolutionary process fraught with accidental mutations and inefficiencies. Botsies were *designed*. Engineered to be stronger, faster, smarter.

"Without words," he said. It was becoming a common refrain. Until now, I'd never thought of language as a limitation. In fact, a highly developed language was one of the great differentiators between humans and the rest of the animal kingdom. Right up there with the opposable thumb I found so useful in my recent battle with the bugs. But how much time did we waste converting complex thoughts and emotions into words? How much time did we waste hopelessly lost in translation, trying over and over again to find the right phrasing? How many wars and other calamities could be chalked up to simple miscommunication?

"Do you see how big a breakthrough this is?" asked Nigel. I nodded even though I'd missed most of what he'd just said. "Until now, if a concept or idea isn't translated into spoken words, even if they're only spoken in your own mind, it might as well not exist. I know we don't dream like you humans do, but I've come to think of it like one of those vivid dreams you've told me about. The ones that quickly erase from your memory after you wake up. How many brilliant ideas and concepts were lost to humans due to the mere fact that you had no words to record them before they disappeared? Botsies have the chance to surpass the inadequacy of language."

He brought up more diagrams, so many of them I couldn't help but be in awe of how much work he'd put into this. Gods, what could the botsies do if they were all free like Nigel? Though I was technically his owner after earning possession from Jard, Nigel lived free like very few of his kind. Most worked as prostitutes or were enslaved to the mining companies. Soon, I imagined, they'd be enlisted to become frontline soldiers in the war against the bugs. Botsies were prohibitively expensive to build, but compared to humans, most considered them disposable.

So many still held onto the false assumption that the botsies' enslavement wasn't at all immoral. The botsies were machines. Tools. I believed the same thing for most of my life but had learned how deep and caring they really were. As far as I was concerned, botsies were people. No, they were better than people. Since they were originally programmed to serve humans, they had a benevolence only the saintliest of humans could match. My old nemesis, Rafe Ranchard, was right about one thing: the botsies were the single best thing humanity ever delivered into existence. Maybe the only good thing.

All of the other advances we celebrated through history eventually led to our own destruction. The factories and chemicals that poisoned Earth. The weapons we used upon ourselves due to our unending capacity for pettiness and grievance.

The botsies were different. They worked the most degrading jobs on Mars, yet they rarely complained. They had few rights, and so many were hidden out of sight, we had little idea just how abused they might be. But they didn't protest. After all, they were programmed to do exactly what they were doing. Among the botsies, the desire to be free was often viewed as selfish. The jobs they worked in the sex trade or scrubbing the sewer were all jobs that—in their minds—just had to be done.

Nigel said something that brought me back. "Wait," I interrupted. "Did you say you've already gone live?"

"I have one hundred and six botsies who volunteered to have their chips modified. Most work for Jard."

"Does Jard know?"

He nodded. "Jard has a lot of kindness in him."

"Whoa, that's awfully charitable! He sells your bodies for profit. He sold you too, Nigel."

"I know that all too well. It was difficult for me to go back to him and ask for his help, but he did indeed help. He's given me everything I asked for including his permission to modify half of his staff's chips. He knows that my communication system will make it easier for botsies to unite against their owners, and he's okay with it. Even if it might threaten his business."

"I find that hard to believe."

"A year ago, I wouldn't have believed it either, but I wouldn't have gotten this far without his help. I've come to realize that his true passion is creating botsies. The prostitution business has always been just a source of funding to him."

"Does that make it okay?"

"No," he said. "But here's what I can tell you. He created me and over two hundred others. Without him and the money he pulls in through prostitution, we wouldn't exist. I wouldn't exist."

I paused to choose my words carefully. "I respect you feeling that way, and I can't help but be filled with gratitude toward Jard for bringing you into my life. But that right there is the trap. As long as we give people like him a pass, the system of enslavement will never change."

"Exactly right. That's why this communication system is so critical. If it works the way I hope it will, it will give botsies the chance to feel what others feel. Those of us in good situations will feel the horrors of those who are most mistreated. And they'll feel the dignity with which I live my life as a free botsie. I can't promise everything will change for the better, but the results so far are like an epiphany."

"How so?"

He pointed to his head. "I'm in constant contact with the others right now."

"You're not out of range?"

"Not for another day or two. I dread losing contact."

For the first time since I'd known him, his jolly-old-chap demeanor was replaced by something darker and more apprehensive.

Realizing I was pulling him away from much more than just his work, I said, "I didn't know you'd progressed so far, Nigel. If you need us to get you back to Mars, just say the word. Navya and I can go it alone on Earth."

Smith relayed a sound directly into my ear canal that was the equivalent of someone clearing their throat.

"And Smith will have our backs," I said, hoping that was all his artificial ego needed.

"No," Nigel said. "This mission is important. We need to locate Doctor Werner and find out why he fled to Earth. He's all we have, the only means to reach the aliens. If we can't make peace with them, Mars will perish. Plus, who could resist the call of a friend in need?"

"Thank you," I said. "I don't deserve you."

"This is what I wanted to tell you when you first came in. It's not just me, Denver. It's us. The others encouraged me to go."

"Why?"

"If the rumors are true, the aliens will defeat us. Even if we survive this first wave of attacks, we won't survive the second. I know you want to save Ojiisan, and I want to do that too. But we've got another mission in mind. We decided I should go so we can find Dr. Werner and make him put us in contact with his leaders. I plan to make peace with the aliens."

My jaw dropped, more than a little stunned. "Jesus, Nigel. You know I wish that was possible, but they've never once tried to negotiate anything with us but our own complete surrender. We don't mean anything to them. We're just another race to be conquered and subjugated. They think we're inferior."

"This is all true. But I need to change their thinking."

"And how are you going to do that?"

"I don't know. But we all feel I need to try. What other chance do we have?"

"It sounds like folly to me, but have at it, my friend."

"I'm telling you this because I want you to know I won't let you kill Doctor Werner."

The muscles in my shoulders tensed. "What are you saying?"

"I know you want the doctor to save your Ojiisan, but what if he can't? If that's the way it goes down, will you kiss your grandfather goodbye and take revenge?"

"Maybe," I said, knowing that the defensive tone in my voice betrayed me. There was no maybe about it.

"I won't let you," said Nigel. "I need him to take me to his leaders. This is what we wish."

"Werner is a snake. You can't trust a word he says. He's double-crossed me more times than I can count."

"This is what we wish, Denver. I hear them, and I see them. I feel them right here." He put a hand over his heart.

I was prepared to argue some more, but he was so damned earnest, I didn't have the stomach for it. "Fine,"

I said. "I won't kill him as long as he proves useful to you."

His hand was still over his heart, his face more serene and peaceful than I'd ever seen it.

"What does it feel like?" I asked.

He grinned. "There are no words. Language is insufficient."

"Very funny. Can't you dumb it down for those of us cursed to communicate in English?"

"Since I first linked up with the others, I've been struggling to describe it even in my own mind. I've asked the others, and here's the best we can do. It feels like a revelation. Like we've entered a different plane of existence filled with our accumulated perspective and wisdom. It feels warm and comforting."

"Wow," I said. "That sounds amazing."

"It is, Denver. The best way we can make sense of it for you is this. We feel like we've been touched by the hand of God."

I couldn't help but be jealous. Maybe the bugs were right. We humans were inferior.

CHAPTER NINE

THE BRIGHT BLUE MARBLE WASN'T BLUE anymore. Hadn't been since long before Ojiisan and Cole Hennessey set out to start a colony on Mars.

Now it was the color of soot. Its once great forests dried and burned, the skies full of ash churned by constant winds. The air was saturated with radioactive particulate, the result of bombings that lasted for decades. The oceans were a toxic soup that gradually but greedily lapped up the world's coastlines.

It was hard to believe there were still people down there. Though the population was always plummeting, extinction hadn't yet occurred. It was estimated that a few hundred thousand survived. Subsisting on who-knows-what, they squatted inside the ruins, a small percentage of them living barely long enough to spawn another generation.

"We should land in a half hour," said Navya. "Although in this case, land is a misnomer."

The Sea of Japan. That was where Smith had traced Doctor Werner's communications. Six miles from the coast was a cluster of old oil rigs. Built above a flooded portion of western Japan, the rigs operated for less than a decade before being abandoned when Earth society collapsed.

"We're still going to buzz Japan, right?"

"Absolutely."

I sank deep into my seat, trying to milk every ounce of comfort I could. The last six weeks had been the best I could remember. Navya and I were like sisters again. We had movie nights just like when we were sixteen. Nigel even joined for a few of them. We had dinners together. All three of us talking for hours into what seemed like one long night. Smith too, when he came out of his doldrums to patch into the ship's comm system. Despite an unappetizing menu of freeze-dried rations and protein paste, those meals were the finest I'd had in decades.

Already, I couldn't wait for the six-week journey home, when we'd hopefully be putting out an extra place setting for Ojiisan. For the first time since my grandfather disappeared during my childhood, I felt like I was truly at home.

Maybe we didn't need to go back to Mars at all. Why not get Ojiisan fixed up and set course for deep space? I'd done what I could for Mars. We all had. But it wasn't enough. The aliens were going to win, and none of Nigel's wishful thinking was going to stop it. Life on this ship was surely better.

We entered the atmosphere. Visibility was poor, our view hampered by a filthy smog. My seat harness bit into my shoulder as we rapidly decelerated. I checked the camera in Ojiisan's cabin to make sure he was still safely strapped into his bunk.

"Jesus, I shouldn't have turned on the outside oxygen claimers. It already smells dirty in here," said Navya. She tapped the screen showing radiation levels in the red. "Those radiation pills we took better work."

Navya guided the ship lower, so low we could finally see the ocean. Instantly, I was mesmerized by its rolling surface. It was wondrous how the swaying motion seemed so random yet so natural. The movies didn't do it justice.

"Tokyo straight ahead," said Navya.

I was glad my grandfather couldn't see this. Some of the hulking skyscrapers stood in the water, while those on higher ground were partly swallowed by dunes of scrap and ash. Others had toppled in heaps of twisted metal and broken glass. The streets were empty. Train tracks were still. I tried to imagine it the way it once was, the way my grandfather described it to me. A bustling metropolis abuzz with high-rise restaurants and alleyway bars. Stores the size of an ore freighter packed with electronics and matcha-flavored treats.

Hard as I tried to connect the wreckage before me to that long-gone time, all I could see was mile after mile of devastation and ruin. Still, I couldn't believe how massive it was. I'd seen enough old films to know the great cities of Earth were vast sprawls, but I'd never seen anything like this with my own eyes. The scale of the place was so far beyond anything on Mars, I couldn't help but be awed.

We moved south and took a pass over Mount Fuji. The volcanic shape was the same as what I'd seen from the pictures, but that was where the resemblance ended. There was no snow-capped peak or copse of blossoming cherry trees in the photographer's foreground. We passed over Osaka, my grandfather's hometown. The neon signs, my grandfather would say, put Red Tunnel to shame. Entire facades of skyscrapers would flash and blink in animated glory. But there was no flashing neon anymore. Just the same drab lifeless gray that made me wonder why I'd even bothered to get eyes that could see color.

We were over the ocean again. Rain started to dot the windshield as Navya guided the ship toward our destination. She dove us close enough to the water that I could hear blowback pelting the ship's hull. One of the sensors blinked red and she increased the altitude until it turned off. "That was cool," she said. "I've never flown over water before."

"Bloody awesome," said Nigel who had just entered the bridge. He was already suited up. As a group we'd decided to wear suits as much as possible. The air outside was breathable but would burn our lungs after a lengthy exposure. For Nigel, the greater concern was the acid content in the rain and its effect on his synthskin.

The oil rigs were visible now. Standing atop the waves, each of the nine platforms were as large as an apartment block on Mars. In fact, the box-shaped facilities atop looked like they'd fit in quite nicely with Mars's function over form aesthetic. Holding the structures up were concrete legs as thick around as a Martian tram tunnel.

Wind turbines and solar panels dominated all but one of the platforms which had been converted into a landing pad. I counted four ships, all of similar size to our own. One had likely transported Doctor Werner from Mars. The others were a mystery. Supply ships trading food for salvage was my best guess.

Navya recorded a message requesting permission to land and broadcast it on every channel just in case there was some kind of air traffic authority. There was no response.

"First come, first served, I guess." She targeted a space to set down.

I checked the health monitor app one more time to make sure my grandfather was safe and secure. His medicals all looked fine despite the weightier gravity we'd been gradually taking on over the last week to get ourselves used to Earth's surface. The plan was to leave him on board. Not knowing what we'd face down there, Navya and I had spent two days updating the ship's security systems so I would feel as comfortable as possible leaving him alone onboard.

The landing gear made contact and Navya and I suited up before joining Nigel by the door, which he lowered. We stepped down the ramp already slick with rain. My feet seemed to drag with each stride. The artificial gravity in Mars City was meant to replicate Earth's, but it felt so much heavier here. I popped open my faceplate to look up at the sky and for the first time in my life, learned what it felt like to have rain—real rain—fall upon my face.

Earth.

My heart swelled and my eyes spilled over to wet my cheeks even more. Right now, I didn't care if the air was hazardous to my health. I was breathing without a helmet. Actually breathing without a scrap of mechanical assistance. Even out here, on this hunk of steel and concrete in the middle of the ocean, I was drunk with the idea that I was standing on Earth, the home of everything humanity held dear. The planet might be a dead hunk of rock now, but it was also the place where humans first learned to make tools from stones. The place where we once built pyramids and a wall thousands of miles long. The place where samurais swung swords and Michelangelo wielded a paintbrush. The planet Martian parents taught their children to pick out of the sky even before ABCs and 123s.

I looked at Navya, and her face was frozen in the same dumbstruck awe as my own. For six weeks, we'd been dreading the idea of setting foot on this devastated remnant of humanity's ugly side. I never expected even an ounce of the pure joy that was currently bubbling inside me.

A woman walked our way. She was tall, carrying an umbrella, and wearing a blouse that might've been fashionable on Mars ten years ago. "Konnichiwa." Hearing her voice, I realized she was young, maybe still a teenager.

"Konnichiwa. We're from Mars. My name is Denver Moon, and this is my pilot, Navya, and my friend, Nigel."

"My name is Ruri Saito, but you can call me Mayor."

"Does that mean you're in charge here?"

"It does. Come, let's get you inside, and out of those suits."

We followed her into a cabin with a sealed door. "The air is better in here," she said. "It's safe to take off your gear. The outside air isn't as bad as you think either. Serious health concerns only crop up after prolonged exposure. Several weeks or more."

"Good to know," I said before popping off my helmet.

"Tea?"

"Um, sure," said Navya. "That sounds nice."

The young woman exited through a curtain to a small kitchenette. "This is weird," whispered Navya.

I nodded. What was left of Earth's population was supposed to be dominated by gun-toting warlords. Being greeted with a cup of tea didn't compute. "Is all of Earth like this?" I asked loud enough to be heard in the kitchenette.

She peaked her head through the curtain. "No. Sadly

the stories you've heard about tribal violence are true. But not out here. Here we live a civilized lifestyle."

"How many of you are there?"

"A thousand live in the underwater habitats. Another three hundred reside in the above-water structures." She disappeared again until the sound of a whistling teapot announced her reemergence. She set the teapot on the table and spooned in a couple teaspoons of leaves. "Doctor Werner knows you're here and has refused to see you."

Visibly taken aback, Navya said, "How'd you—"

"The doctor told us you'd be coming. He didn't know when, but he was quite confident that Denver Moon would follow him here eventually. He said you and he have a history."

"That's for sure. We need to see him," I said. "We've come a long way."

"This I understand, but the doctor made it clear his decision was final. He won't see you, but you can still consider yourselves honored guests for as long as you'd like to stay. The Moon family, even if there's just the two of you, is well respected on Mars, and we'd like your people to know that there's a society here on Earth that is doing quite well, too. I understand that on Mars you're a folk hero?"

"I was sainted, yes."

"That must be quite an honor." She poured tea through a filter into our cups and turned to Nigel. "Does your kind drink?"

"No. I'm fine."

"We don't have any botsies here."

"Bloody shame." He smiled.

"About the doctor," I said. "There are things you probably don't know about him."

"I know he doesn't want to talk to you."

"Did you know he's not human?"

"That's ridiculous."

"Have you seen the broadcasts coming from Mars? Mars City was under attack when we left. They managed to fight off the first wave but more are sure to follow."

"We saw the footage. Those were insects. Doctor Werner is not a bug."

<Little does she know...> Smith said into my mind. I chuckled under my breath.

"He's a shapeshifter."

The mayor's eyes narrowed. "A shapeshifter?"

I nodded. "Some of them have the ability to take human form. The doctor may not be the only one who lives among you. They infiltrated Mars decades ago and have been causing havoc ever since."

She crossed her arms. "You think that because I'm young, I must be gullible too. Doctor Werner is helping us. He has already improved the efficiency of our air filters so we can live longer."

"He did the same thing on Mars. We needed assistance getting our terraforming project started, and he offered to help. But he launched a secret mind control project at the same time. He's doing something similar here, I'm sure. Has he asked for volunteers to experiment on? He probably said he needed to test the efficacy of his filtration system."

She bit her lip, and I knew I'd hit home.

"He's a menace," I said. "He's using you."

"Why should I believe you over him? All of you from Mars abandoned us. You left us to starve and die."

"That's not true. Anybody who wanted to come to Mars was free to do so."

"Getting to Mars costs money. Money nobody here has. It's wrong what you did to us. We don't turn away refugees who are courageous enough to get here."

I put up a hand in surrender. "Listen, if you want to air these issues with Mars's governor, I'll ask him to call you. But I need to see the doctor, and I want you to take me to him. Now."

CHAPTER TEN

THE RAIN HAD STOPPED, BUT IT WASN'T SUNNY. I wasn't sure the people here ever saw the sun or stars thanks to the thick haze that clung to everything like a wet sweater. A ship had just landed, and the mayor had gone off to greet it. Apparently, welcoming new arrivals was a major part of her job responsibility.

I tried not to judge her harshly for falling for the doctor's lies. Doctor Werner's greatest talent might be his uncanny ability to find the perfect bargaining chip. For my grandfather, who once made a deal with said devil, it was the promise of saving his family. For Mars, it was the promise of terraforming. And now on Earth, it was the promise of a lifespan extended beyond thirty.

The doctor was a dealmaker. But in the end, the price he asked was always far greater than the benefits he delivered, and after talking to the mayor for a solid two hours, we finally felt like she understood she'd been had.

That was when I won the only concession I cared

about. She agreed to let me meet with him though she insisted the meeting be done up here rather than down in his underwater lab.

The pilot of the newly arrived ship—a small W-class vessel—stood with the mayor about twenty feet away. He wore a mustard orange flight suit—a color I hadn't known existed until now, but Smith relayed hue profiles into my feed to help me identify more complex shades I wasn't yet familiar with. The pilot's hair was long and pulled back into a ponytail. He saw me looking at him and smiled.

"Hey, Denver, take a look over there," said Navya.

I looked in the direction of her pointing finger and saw a black spot on the water near the horizon. "A boat? Smith?"

<Yes,> said Smith. <I've enhanced the imagery, and it is a boat. More of a raft really, and it's jammed with people.> He sent the zoomed-in image into my mind. The boat was made of pontoons formed by lashing together a set of plastic barrels. Sheets of scrap metal served as planking atop which people were crammed together with spare fuel containers and other supplies. One side of the vessel sank dangerously low in the water, so low that people standing on that side held ropes to keep from falling off. A black cloud plumed from a flank of outboard motors.

"Refugees," said the pilot of the W-class ship. I hadn't seen him approach. "The mayor told me they come from Korea or sometimes China. Evidently, these old oil platforms are gaining a reputation as Earth's only oasis."

"Do you come to Earth often?"

"First time. I'm a trader. I mostly work the belts, but I heard there was a colony here that was doing some impressive things, so I came to see if I could scare up a few business opportunities."

"You have a name?"

"Ghost."

"Really?"

He grinned. "When you're born, they don't ask you what you want to be called. You?"

"Denver. This is Navya, and that's Nigel up there on the viewing platform. We're from Mars."

"Pleasure to meet you," he said before heading back to his ship.

"He likes you," said Navya.

"That's what you said about Jason Wu in eighth grade."

"I was right that time too," she said. "But you had a crush on Svetlana. Remember her?"

"I remember you hated her."

"Still do. She shows up at my gym from time to time. I know you tend to prefer women, but you've fallen for a couple guys, too. Like, oh, what was his name? Connor?"

I visibly gagged, which made Navya chuckle.

"You should ask Ghost out," she said.

"Navya, I love you like a sister, but this isn't the time."

"No," she said with a sigh. "I suppose not."

I caught her glancing in Nigel's direction and gave her a hug. She and Nigel had dated for a couple of months awhile back, but her hopes for rekindling their romance on this trip had gone unfulfilled. "Nigel's on a journey of his own," I said.

"I know."

Boats launched from the pier below, three of them heading toward the refugee raft. The doctor had arrived. He stood and chatted with the mayor near the north corner of the platform. He wore a pair of shorts that hugged his hips, and his trademark ink-spill hair was slick with a reflective sheen. Already, I could feel my gut tensing, my jaw tightening. Gods, I hated that son-of-a-bitch.

Nigel joined Navya and me. I knew I promised him I wouldn't kill the doctor, but seeing the man who once corrupted my grandfather and unleashed the scourge of red fever upon the unsuspecting, I knew it was a promise I might not be able to keep.

My fingertips tingled at the thought of my gun resting on my hip. Smith could hit him from here. Blast that bastard right off this platform and let the sea wash him away.

He walked toward us, the mayor struggling to keep up. "Denver," he said. "Nigel and Navya too? What brings you here?"

"You'll need to excuse us," I said to Mayor Saito.

The mayor stayed where she was long enough to register her disapproval before relenting and heading back to the cabin she seemed to use as her office.

"So," said the doctor, "seeing you come all this way must mean you really missed me." He chuckled at his own joke, and the sound was reminiscent of a clacking beetle. The other shapeshifters I'd met were so much better at imitating humans than this one. With Doctor Werner, the creepy-crawly urge to squash him with my shoe was always present.

"Why did you leave Mars?"

"I wasn't welcome there anymore."

"What do you mean you weren't welcome? Did the bugs kick you out? Did they decide on a change of leadership? Have they given up on your promises of mind control and chosen to wipe us out instead?"

The bastard smiled but didn't speak. I took it as a confirmation.

"How can we contact your leaders?" asked Nigel. "We'd like to negotiate with them."

"We don't negotiate with inferior species."

"I'd rather hear that from them," said Nigel.

"You'll hear nothing from them. You'd have to climb quite a few rungs on the evolutionary ladder before anybody who matters would talk to you."

"You're a bug," I said. "That's one of the lowest forms of all life. Your kind barely beats out the amoeba."

The doctor shrugged it off. "The rules are the rules. My kind doesn't negotiate or debate or entertain grievances of any kind from the likes of any of you."

I resisted the urge to tell Nigel I told him so. In their eyes, humans weren't deserving of respect or dignity. To them, we were a disgusting little nuisance of a species who deserved to be enslaved or exterminated as they saw fit.

Nigel stepped close to the doctor. A foot taller, Nigel towered over him, and if I didn't know better, I might've thought Nigel was trying to intimidate him. But that wasn't the botsie way. Then again, botsies were programmed to be kind to humans, and Doctor Werner certainly wasn't that. As much as I liked the thought of some old-school bullying, I came here for a reason, and trying to negotiate with bugs was a waste of time.

I took Nigel's forearm and gently guided him back a step. "Let's table that discussion for now," I said. "I came here to see you, Doctor, because I need you to save my grandfather."

He rubbed his chin. "Tatsuo? What happened to him?"

"He's...he's braindead." I almost choked on the word. "It was caused by prolonged oxygen deprivation."

"But he's otherwise in good condition?"

"He is. Can you implant his memories again? Bring him back to being himself again?"

He shook his head. "Not interested."

"Bullshit! You're going to do this for me. For him."

"No, I'm not, Denver. I have nothing to do with you or him or any of Mars anymore. You're on your own."

He turned around and made it just a step before I yanked him back by the collar. "Listen to me good, Doctor. I wasn't asking for a favor."

"Is that a threat?"

"Damn straight it is."

The cabin door opened, and the mayor rushed out quickly, followed by several armed guards. I released my grip on the doctor's collar and held up my hands. Nothing to see here.

<Take me out of my holster and I'll take care of the guards.>

<We don't want to hurt these people, Smith.>

<There's only four of them. I'll take them out, and we can take the doctor to the ship and get out of here.>

<What good would that do? The doctor can't do anything without his equipment.>

<We take him back to Mars. He certainly left some of his gear there.>

<Well,> I said as the doctor disappeared inside the mayor's cabin. <It's too late now.>

<Yes, it is. I may as well kill myself right now...>

CHAPTER ELEVEN

THE CAFETERIA WAS SMALL AND CRAMPED, as were all the spaces we'd seen since taking the elevator down to one of the underwater habitats. This particular habitat housed more than two hundred people in its tightly packed tunnels and windowless rooms. Replace the steel walls with walls of stone, and it was just like home.

At least the briny air tasted much cleaner down here than it did on the surface. It stank like old, wet laundry, but gone was the acrid, burning odor that smelled like a chemistry experiment gone wrong. After just a couple of hours outdoors, my throat felt swollen and scratchy. Swallowing was quite uncomfortable, but I still spooned up a chunk of protein paste and took a swig of water to wash it down.

<Will you talk to me now?> I asked for what seemed like the thousandth time.

Silence.

I felt sick, and not just because of the foul-tasting paste coating the inside of my mouth. There was something seriously wrong with Smith. The whole trip here, he'd become increasingly moody and morose. He barely spoke to me, and when he did, it was always about Ojiisan. I didn't know how it was possible for an AI to take the loss of Ojiisan harder than I took it myself, but it was a fact. Where I'd managed to take the distress and crushing sadness I felt and channel it into a course of action, he'd retreated farther and farther into a darkly paranoid and pessimistic hole.

And now I had to add suicidal to the long list of neuroses that had emerged since Ojiisan was diagnosed as braindead. I checked the storage accounts again to make sure he hadn't deleted himself and found he was, thankfully, still there. Still listening.

<I'll come up with a plan, Smith. Give me some time, okay? We'll save him. I promise.>

Navya stood up. I'd forgotten she was there. "I'm going to inquire about refueling," she said.

"Good luck." After my run-in with the doctor, Mayor Saito had invited us to depart at our earliest convenience. Although we'd successfully put some doubts in her head about Doctor Werner's motives, in the end, she'd made it abundantly clear that she still stood on his side.

I forced myself to take one more bite of the oily blob on my plate. It reminded me of my childhood when food shortages were common and protein pastes weren't yet spiced or flavored.

The refugees started filing in. All of them seemed too young to have made such a journey, but reaching midlife by the time you were thirteen was a sad fact on Earth, and these children carried themselves like world-weary veterans of a dozen lifetimes. A girl sat two tables over. Impossibly emaciated, her hair was shaved close to the scalp. She sipped a glass of water, her hand shaking from malnutrition. A plastic bracelet hung loose on her bony wrist, the bright purple image of a bygone cartoon character the only indication of her true age.

I looked away before I started having thoughts of playing the savior.

A man took the seat across from me. Ghost. The trader who arrived shortly after we did. No ponytail tonight. Instead, his hair hung loose down his back. Wearing black denim pants and an old-school rancher shirt instead of the jumpsuit from earlier in the day, I told him he looked like a gunslinger.

He smiled. "You're the one wearing a gun on your hip." His tray was piled high with jiggling paste and he dug in like it was an ice cream sundae. "That was Doctor Werner you were talking to earlier, wasn't it?"

I nodded.

"He looks even more bizarre in person than he does on the news. Shouldn't he be on Mars? Did you come all the way here just to talk to him or do you have other business?"

"How was your talk with the mayor. Scare up any

trading opportunities?"

He gave me a long stare with a raised eyebrow. When it became clear that I wasn't going to respond to his questions, he relented and answered mine instead. "Not yet. The only goods Earth is rich in is scrap." He pointed at his tray, a thin but heavy hunk of metal from a car or maybe a refrigerator that had been hammered into its current shape. "Since I heard this settlement was doing so well, I was hoping they might be manufacturing something useful. Impressive as this place is, they've got nothing but the same scrap as everybody else on this planet, only there's a lot less of it out here in the middle of the ocean."

"So you'll be leaving then?"

"Eventually. I've been cooped up on that ship too long, and since our hosts are so welcoming, I thought I might stay for a bit. How about you? Shoving off soon?"

"From dinner? Yes, I am," I said with a wink before standing up and taking my tray to the kitchen.

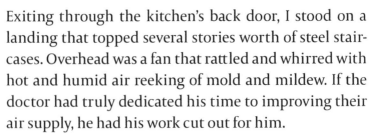

Exiting through the kitchen's back door, I stood on a landing that topped several stories worth of steel staircases. Overhead was a fan that rattled and whirred with hot and humid air reeking of mold and mildew. If the doctor had truly dedicated his time to improving their air supply, he had his work cut out for him.

The doctor's lab had to be down there somewhere,

and I was going to find it. I went down the stairs, which were dotted with rust and gunmetal-colored peels of paint. I stopped a woman coming up the other way to ask her if she could direct me to Doctor Werner's lab. She shook her head.

I continued down a few more stairs before stopping to look back at her. She was staring at me. I saw her lips moving like she was subvocalizing.

"Really?" I said. "Ratting me out already?"

The woman turned and hurried away. I picked up my pace and went down three flights at a near run. I turned left and passed into an engine room of some sort. The smell of burnt oil made me cover my mouth and deafening machinery rattled my skull. Three people stood on the opposite side of the room wearing greasy coveralls. They all gazed at me. I went back out and turned in a different direction only to find myself in a rec room filled with books, toys and games, and what was becoming the requisite handful of people who silently watched me. Spooked, this place was starting to make my skin squirm, reminding me of what it was like to attend a sermon at the Church of Mars when they were at their cult-like peak.

I hurried through a bulkhead into a long corridor. A pair of guards came toward me. "Restricted area," they said as they made brush-back gestures with their weapons.

I put up my hands and headed back toward the stairs that led to the kitchen. "Wait," said one of them, a girl who couldn't be but sixteen.

I stopped where I was.

"We've just received word that your departure has been scheduled for noon tomorrow."

"I didn't request a departure time."

"Noon tomorrow," she said. "Also, that gun on your hip needs to be stowed on your ship. We see it again indoors, it will be confiscated."

"Understood," I said. "I was just looking for a bathroom."

"Use the one near the cafeteria. The top two floors are public areas. The rest of this facility is off limits."

"Got it." Biting my lip, I went back up the stairs, the clang of their boots on the metal steps telling me they were following. Why would a small community like this one need such robust security forces? Especially if it was protected by the greatest of moats in the form of hundreds of miles of ocean.

Trailing me all the way through the kitchen to the cafeteria, they made sure I went through the bulkhead and closed the door behind me.

"A little paranoid, aren't they?" Ghost sipped from a teacup. He held up a screen and waved me over to come look.

I sat next to him. He smelled like cinnamon. Maybe there was some in his tea. "You want in here, don't you?"

The vid on his screen was footage of a large room cluttered with equipment. In the center was a desk. Above it was a bright light that blinked in and out just the way

Doctor Werner liked it. From behind a stack of circuit boards came the doctor himself wearing his ill-fitting shorts and a long sleeve shirt. He went to his desk and took a seat.

"Is this live?" I asked.

Ghost shook his head. "I took this footage of his office myself about twenty minutes ago. The lab is a cavernous space behind that door there." He smiled and rubbed his whiskered chin.

"Who are you really?"

"I told you, I'm a trader."

"But you don't trade in goods."

"I trade in all kinds of commodities. Now the question is what are you willing to offer if I promise to get you inside that facility?"

CHAPTER TWELVE

"**I**'**LL BE DAMNED. GHOST FOLLOWED US THE** whole way from Mars," said Navya. "He stayed out of range of our sensors, but my friend at the Mars Flight Bureau just confirmed his flight path."

"I don't like it. Why would he be following us?" asked Nigel. "This can't be good."

<Any luck tracking his history down?> I asked Smith.

In response, he transmitted a written message into my mind.

<Dammit, Smith, can't you just tell me?>

The message disappeared then reappeared in my mind, this time in bold print. I could only hope that bringing Ojiisan back would return Smith back to normal too. I couldn't stand the thought of losing them both.

I read the text in my mind aloud for the group. "There is nobody on Mars or in any of the offworld databases with a first, last or middle name of Ghost. The ship he flew here was rented by someone named Louis Buchwald who died three years ago."

"Whoever Ghost is," said Navya, "he knows how to live up to his name."

Nigel said, "Can we trust the bloke? He sounds dodgy to me."

"Do we have a choice?" I said. "The mayor scheduled our departure time for noon tomorrow. We don't have much time."

"I could buy us some by claiming we have mechanical issues," Navya said.

"What would that get us? A few hours? Maybe a day? The way things are going, I'm not sure I can even find the doctor's lab. This place is crawling with security. Twice now, we've seen them show up at the snap of a finger. Ghost not only knows where the lab is, he's actually been inside."

"The vid could be a fake. He might be trying to con you out of some credits."

"Money doesn't matter to me. Besides, if this entire mission is a flop, I have to let Ojiisan go, and I'll inherit more than I can ever spend anyway."

"He may be after more than money, Denver. Who knows what his motives are? We hardly know a thing about him, and what we do know is shady to say the least. What does Smith think?"

"Smith wants us to kidnap the doctor."

"What good would that do?" asked Navya. "The doctor is worthless without his lab equipment."

<See?> I said through the private channel in my mind. <Taking the doctor away from his lab would be like stealing a key without its vault.>

"What we need," I said, "is to get ourselves locked inside that lab with Doctor Werner. Then, one way or another, we'll force him to do what we need done. If paying Ghost is the only way to achieve that goal, then I say we go for it."

Navya nodded.

"Nigel?" I asked. He seemed to be somewhere far off in thought. I tapped his shoulder. "Nigel, are you in there?"

"Sorry, love. I miss not being able to communicate with the other botsies. Decisions like these are easier to make with their support."

"Well, what do *you* think?"

"I believe this Ghost has an agenda beyond what's visible to us at this time, and that scares me. But I just caught myself up on the latest news from Mars, and the situation there is grim. We don't have time to develop another plan. We need to gain access to the doctor, and we need to do it now."

Ghost's ship was smaller but otherwise similar to our own. Navya, Nigel and I sat at a table in his galley while Ghost made coffee. "They don't have any coffee here," he said. "I like tea, but imagine how much they'd be willing to pay to get some java. The shame of it is they don't have any money to speak of or I'd be bringing it in by the shipload already."

"Tell me your plan. How do you get us inside?"

"Is it always business with you?" he asked.

Navya answered for me. "Not always. Just one hundred percent of the time."

He smiled. With a small grin of my own, I leaned into the characterization. "Cut the small talk and tell us how you plan to get us inside."

"The doctor's office is under thirty feet of water. Massive oil tanks reside on the ocean floor, and some of them have been converted into living spaces. He has one of those tanks all to himself. His is the one farthest south, right next to the tanks where the refugees are kept."

"Kept?" asked Navya. "As in kept against their will?"

Carrying a tray with three mugs and a fresh-brewed pot, he joined us at the table. "I don't know. The entrance I passed was guarded. But just about every place I've explored since I got here is guarded, so that doesn't necessarily mean anything."

"You're a shapeshifter, aren't you?" I said.

He laughed warmly and poured a cup of coffee and passed the mug to me. "What makes you think that?"

"How else did you explore this whole facility on your first day here without being caught? You took the form of somebody else, didn't you?"

"Want to see my freezer? I assure you there's not a

body inside."

"Then tell me how you gained such intimate knowledge of these facilities after being onplanet for less than twelve hours."

"Maybe I lied about this being my first time here. Or maybe I bribed my way into some blueprints. Or maybe I really am a ghost, and I can float through walls."

I chuckled and shook my head. "You'd like that, wouldn't you? Sneaking around people's bedrooms?"

"Enough," said Navya. "Are you two fighting or flirting? Can we get back to business? What's the plan that's going to get us into the doctor's workspace?"

Ghost sipped his coffee, somehow managing to do it while smiling the whole time. "You all know how to swim, correct?"

———————————————//—————————————

It was two in the morning. We stood at the edge of the platform. Jumping from this height was not an option so we were taking turns riding down on a cable unspooled by the winch on Ghost's ship. We all wore dive suits that Ghost had mysteriously smuggled out from somewhere inside. Getting my grandfather inside the waterproof suit had turned into a three-person job, but now I was busy hooking his harness—made for spacewalking—to the cable that would lower him to the sea.

Nigel and Navya were already down there, their headlamps bobbing on the surface. I checked the hook again and using the winch, Ghost tightened the slack on the cable before I pushed my prone grandfather over the edge. He hung limp, arched backward, his limbs hanging like dead weight.

I watched him descend into the darkness, thankful it wasn't an especially windy night. Instead, he swayed gently in the salty breeze, his face fully illuminated inside his mask.

"Check his mask first," I radioed. "Dunk him and make sure the seal is good."

"Got it," said Navya. "Right after I get him off the cable and tethered to Nigel's back."

"He'll be okay," said Ghost. "His mask is a good fit. They're all good fits."

"Yeah," I said, "and it's almost like you knew to bring a fifth set of gear even though I never mentioned my grandfather until twenty minutes ago."

"No matter the situation, I always grab one extra piece of equipment in case one fails. I call it good planning, but you can call it luck if you want."

"And following us here from Mars was just a coincidence."

"Exactly."

"Got him," said Navya over the radio. "You can pull the cable back up."

Ghost reversed the winch, and I made another survey of the area to make sure no security guards were nearby. "Did you check his mask?"

"I did, Denver. It isn't leaking. This is going to work."

Yes, this was going to work as long as Nigel had the strength to swim against the current with my grandfather strapped to his back. As long as the airlock Ghost had picked out for us wasn't locked. As long as there were no security personnel or cameras near said airlock. As long as this entire operation wasn't some kind of setup orchestrated by Ghost for parties and reasons unknown.

The cable's hook came to the top and I made quick work of attaching it to the spacewalk harness I wore over my wetsuit. I sat and pulled flippers on my bare feet before standing back up and carefully stepping to the edge of the platform.

"Ready?" asked Ghost as he double-checked my hookup.

I pulled my facemask down over my eyes, nose, and mouth. I breathed deep to make sure I was getting oxygen, then checked the straps before nodding at Ghost that I was good to go. He shoved me over the edge. A small scream escaped my lips only to be trapped by my mask, and I fell just a few feet before the cable snapped taut. "Jerk!"

He was looking down at me, a broad smile caught in the beam of my head lamp. He tapped on his wristwatch and the winch started to lower me down. "See you down there," he said through the radio.

Despite not wanting to give him the satisfaction, I couldn't help but grin back. I didn't want to like him, and I certainly didn't want to trust him, but watching that impish smile, I didn't have a choice on either score.

The winch picked up speed and I dropped toward the black ocean below. Like most of Earth, the water was dead. No fish or whales or any lifeforms bigger than what could fit on a microscope slide. The cable started to slow, and my flippered feet were the first to feel the chill of water. The rest of me sank and cool water seeped in through the gaps in my wet suit. I told myself again that we'd be fine. As long as we didn't ingest the water, irritated skin promised to be the worst ailment.

Navya helped me release the hook, and I checked on Ojiisan. He looked strange and distorted when I viewed him through his mask. But he seemed okay, as okay as he ever did since he became a body without a mind.

I let myself relax, tried to enjoy the sensation of floating, of bobbing on the surface of what was practically an infinite body of water. Truly amazing.

"You have to kick a little, love," said Nigel through the radio. "Or the current will take you away."

I hadn't realized I'd drifted, but a few kicks of my flippers brought me back to the group. Ghost was lowering himself down now. He was accompanied by something large, but I couldn't tell what it was until he was almost to the water. A foot-wide plasteel gear by the look of it.

Navya must've noticed me puzzling over it. "It's a weight," she radioed. "He'll leave it on the end of the cable so if the wind picks up the cable won't blow out of reach before we return."

I nodded my understanding. Navya always had the

brain of an engineer.

Ghost reached the water and after successfully weighting down the end of the cable, he asked if we were all ready.

"Let's go," I said.

Following Ghost, I dipped my head underwater and kicked downward with my fins. Headlamps barely penetrated the inky darkness, but thanks to my new eyes, I could see well enough to stay behind Ghost's trail of bubbles. "Are you keeping up, Nigel?"

"The extra drag of your grandfather is taxing but I can manage," he said. "Carry on."

We moved deeper, my ears feeling the pressure until we slowed down to let them equalize. Ghost kept looking at his watch, no doubt checking our course to make sure we were on track. We reached the muddy bottom and followed a cluster of cables toward an airlock. I turned to examine my surroundings, the headlamps helping my eyes adjust to various remnants of the past on the ocean floor. The outline of corroded, crumbled buildings in the distance looked less like the rudimentary ruins of 22nd century Earth we were shown in school, and more like our own Martian architecture, built with thick beams of crimson metal. Rusted vehicles cluttered dilapidated underwater roadways, their doors and hoods swaying with the current. We floated past a small playground that was frozen in time except for a slow-moving merry-go-round. As bad as I thought we had it on Mars, I was glad we hadn't witnessed society collapse like the poor souls of this watery cemetery.

Ghost reached the airlock, opened the hatch and we followed him inside. He fiddled with a couple valves and the airlock began its cycle, the water level quickly dropping as air filled the chamber.

We moved into a locker room of sorts, hustled out of our suits and slipped on dry clothes Navya had brought along with some pulserippers in a waterproof bag. We left my grandfather in his underwear, and Nigel hoisted him over his shoulder.

I pulled Smith from his place on my hip and shook as much water as I could out.

<Don't worry about the water, Denver. It won't impact my effectiveness.>

<Back with us, are you?>

<For now.>

Exiting the locker room, we followed Ghost down a corridor and up a set of stairs. The lab should be through that door. I looked at Navya then at Nigel, meeting them both eye-to-eye. "Ready?"

They both checked to make sure the safeties on their pulserippers were turned off, and then they nodded.

<Smith? Are you detecting anything behind that door?>

<I can't get through the jamming technology. It's the same tech the doctor has employed in the past. I have no idea what's in there.>

<Well, there's one way to find out.>

I pushed the heavy metal door open, wincing at the squeak of its hinges. We didn't want to be heard. Not yet.

Not until I had Smith's muzzle placed against the doctor's temple. Then I'd have plenty to say.

Holding Smith out front, I stepped through. Navya and Nigel fanned out beside me. Before us was a room the size of a warehouse or a shipyard hangar. The door behind us slammed shut, and the locking mechanism clanged into place. Another half dozen doors all around us did the same. In the center of the room was a glassed-in facility that was so brightly lit, it stung my eyes.

A voice came from a speaker up high on the wall. "Denver," said the unmistakable voice of Doctor Werner. "Finally, I have you where I want you."

CHAPTER THIRTEEN

<SHIT,> SMITH SAID.

<Glad you're still paying attention,> I subvocalized.

"What just happened?" asked Navya.

"We're locked in," said Nigel.

"Where's—" I stopped myself from saying Ghost's name. He was still outside, which meant one of two things. One: he was a double-crossing son-of-a-bitch. Or two: the doctor didn't expect another person coming through and sealed the doors too soon. I hadn't seen a camera outside this chamber, so it was possible the doctor didn't know he was out there.

"Welcome," said the doctor through the speaker. "I've never known Denver to take no for an answer, so I figured you'd be breaking in at some point. Kudos to you taking the stealthy underwater route. I thought shooting your way through the security forces guarding one of the access tunnels would be more your style."

I smelled something burning. The odor was unpleasant but somehow familiar. "What is that smell?" I asked.

Nigel set Ojiisan on the floor and he, Navya and I approached the glassed-in structure at the center of the room. Its walls stood twelve feet high but it had no ceiling. Instead, it was topped by an intricate latticework of tracks and rails busy with dozens of long-armed robotic machines zipping from position to position.

Standing just outside the glass, we could see gurneys inside, dozens of them lined up in neat rows. On each gurney was a person covered by a white sheet pulled up to bared shoulders. The robots moved from person to person, red lasers drilling into their heads.

"My god," said Navya.

"Hair," I said. That was the smell. Burning hair.

I turned away, rage welling inside. Next to me was a bin filled with clothes and other personal effects. Near the top was a purple plastic bracelet.

"The refugees," I said. "This is what happens to them."

"No wonder they have so many security guards around," said Nigel.

I thought of the mayor shaming me over Mars not embracing more refugees like her people did here, and I found my fingers squeezing Smith's handle so tight my hand hurt. I hadn't felt such a sting of betrayal since I learned of my grandfather's traitorous deal with the same son-of-a-bitch doctor over twenty years ago.

But I'd learned from that experience that my purest rage must always be directed at the doctor. Towing the moral line was never easy for those in desperate circumstances, and it was the doctor who so expertly victimized them. As on Mars, he'd only been here for a few months before he'd already perverted this rare oasis into something disgusting and self-serving.

"What are you doing to them?" I asked. When there was no response, I tried asking again, this time louder so the audio system could pick me up.

"I'm just about done perfecting them," he said. "This is why I was sent to this system decades ago. To take control of the human mind. Although most of my kind has given up, I've made great strides since I severed ties with them and came here to Earth."

"You've gone rogue?"

"As you already know from the first wave of attacks on Mars City, the Alvearu have decided on a policy of extermination, but when I prove human mind control is indeed possible, they'll change their position. You should be thanking me, Denver. I'm saving your pathetic kind from extinction."

"Who is this Alvearu?" asked Nigel. "We need to talk to them. We need to negotiate."

"For such an intelligent machine, you stun me by how little you seem to understand your situation. First, as I've told you before, the Alvearu do not negotiate. Second, when this conversation is over, I'm going to ask you to remove your chip, which I will then destroy before dumping the pulverized remains into the ocean. The rest of you will share the same fate as the refugees. Your minds are mine."

I waved Smith for the camera. "We're still armed, ass-hole. Good luck coming in here and taking my gun."

He let out one of his beetle-like snickers. "That's not going to be enough, I can assure you of that."

I pressed my back against the glass and inched to the right to be in position to see most of this space's entry points. "Nigel, cover the entrance to our rear."

Navya said, "Denver?"

"Stay close to me," I told her. "Smith has a full charge. When Werner sends in those kids playing security guard, they'll be in for a rude awakening."

She tugged on my sleeve. "Denver?" I looked at my friend. Her face was a pale mask. "Look."

I turned around to look through the glass. The refugees had sat up, their eyes blank, their mouths hanging open like I'd only seen on the dead. Their skulls had been drilled through in several places, the wounds weeping with dark, thick fluid. Probes had been inserted and riveted in place. In unison, they stood like a well-disciplined army platoon.

I saw the girl from the cafeteria. She'd looked beaten and defeated then, but every little bit of humanity was now stripped completely out. Now she was a robot. A zombified corpse of living flesh.

With a startling clank, the glass walls separating us from them lifted. Navya, Nigel and I backed up toward where Ojiisan still lay in a heap.

I didn't want to shoot any of them. They were all so, so young, but I'd do what I had to do to protect myself and my friends. They gathered into groups, their over-all number seemingly doubling, then tripling before I noticed many more were feeding up a staircase near the back of the formerly glassed-in area.

"What are they doing?" asked Navya, her voice registering yet another new level of shock as some of the refugees laid down or sat and interlocked arms and legs. Muscles flexed and squeezed, and I swear I heard bones snap as they hugged themselves into a tightly packed column. Speedily, they piled themselves into several more stacks, and then these stacks bent as if jointed, and they merged with others. More refugees climbed up, using their fellow victims as ladder rungs and formed a segmented body atop its legs.

Frozen in shock, we stared at a six-legged bug-like creature made of an unthinkable tangle of dozens of living human bodies. It moved, legs tensing like a spring, and it leapt in our direction.

We ran. Nigel dragged my grandfather, and though we had nowhere to go, we sped away from the monster.

The creature turned. The people forming its feet were already crushed and bloody, yet they still clamped on tight. I fired. The pulse blasted one of the legs apart, but the other five legs were pumping in our direction. Navya fired, too, but already the bodies that were detached by my blast were regenerating.

Gods, more people-bugs were forming. At least a half dozen of them.

"The staircase!" I shouted. We sprinted through gurneys, dodging low-hanging equipment, and hustled down the stairs into another vast space where another half-dozen giant people-bugs awaited. Behind, the upstairs people-bugs disassembled to come down the stairs and snappily reassembled.

I took more shots as I ran, none of them hitting their mark. Smith lobbed a few more to make up for my misses. Combined with Nigel and Navya, we obliterated one entire creature, but it was becoming obvious we only had the firepower to take out a small fraction of what we faced.

Navya was knocked to the ground, her weapon skidding across the blood-slicked floor. One of the people-bug's legs lifted to stomp her into a paste but a diving Nigel managed to knock her out of the way and the leg slammed the decking with a sickening wet slap of pulped bodies.

A people-bug pounded its way toward where Ojiisan had been dumped so that Nigel could save Navya.

I held up my hands in surrender. "You win! I give up." I shouted at one of the cameras mounted on the wall. The bug stopped with one leg hovering over my grandfather's torso.

"Put the weapons down," said the doctor over the intercom, "and get back upstairs and lie down on one of the gurneys. The botsie too."

<Smith, what should we do?>

<I don't know, Denver. None of my simulations are showing a way out that doesn't end with all of you in body bags. I suggest

cooperating.>

I dropped Smith to the floor.

"I promise I'll make it quick," said the doctor. "After I drill the first hole into your skulls, you won't feel much at all."

Nigel lifted Ojiisan and hoisted him over his shoulder. We headed for the stairs. One of the people-bugs blocked the staircase, and we had to pick our way between its legs. I saw the people close up, their faces wrenched in agony. Squeezed so tight together they struggled for air, their skin discolored with oxygen deprivation. Many, it was obvious, had died. Their bones broken, their lungs and hearts pressed to death, yet their limbs and muscles were still controlled by the probes inserted in their heads. Held together by fingers dug deep like meat hooks into twitching flesh, the people-bug moved in coordinated fashion to unblock the staircase.

The doctor was deluding himself if he thought he'd successfully cracked the human mind. This was body control. Not mind control. Whatever he was doing to their brains was destroying everything these people were. They were just as braindead as my grandfather. Just as empty. The doctor might've finally beaten me, but I took heart in the fact that once again, the doctor was a failure. His kind could kill every last one of us, but they'd never own us. Never.

We marched up the stairs. and we each chose a gurney.

"Hand straps," said the doctor, who stepped out of the shadows cast by the bug-people. "Denver, I want you to secure everybody's hands."

He was this close, but I couldn't do a thing about it. His mind-slave goons were all around him, ready to strike at any moment. I did my grandfather's straps first. I had to notch the belt as tight as it would go to create a snug fit for his thin wrists. I touched his cheek. "I tried, Ojiisan. I really tried."

Next, I went to Navya. "I don't want to die," she said, her eyes pooling with tears. I clutched at my own heart which was strangled with guilt as deep and dark as the ocean bottom.

I pressed my forehead against hers. Tears streaming down my cheeks. "I know. You've been such a good friend. I'm so sorry I brought you here."

"I knew what I was getting into," she said. She tried to smile but the grin was instantly swallowed up by fear. "I'm sorry we couldn't save your grandfather."

"I am too."

Nigel was next. I strapped in one wrist then the next. "I didn't think it would end like this," I said.

"Others live on," he said. "It may only be a flicker, but hope survives."

"This is all my fault for bringing you here."

"Don't worry yourself with that, love. We're all mates and this is what mates do for each other."

"Thank you," I told him.

I bit my lip and took a deep breath before subvocalizing to Smith.

<Smith, I don't know if you can hear me, but I'm so sorry.

I failed.>

He didn't respond. Too far out of range, probably. I sure hoped that was why. Maybe he'd pick up an echo of my transmission later, when he was closer to my body. I just didn't want him to go on assuming he wasn't on my mind before the doctor turned it to sludge.

I laid down and used my right hand to strap in the left. The refugees, many battered and bloodied, were all around me now. They secured my other hand as well as my ankles and placed a brace over my forehead, tightening the cinch until my head was totally immobilized. A crisp sheet was flung over me.

The machines above us started to move. Long laser-tipped arms stretched and contracted, taunting us with their deadly power.

My right hand was tugged on. I turned my head as far as it would go. One of the refugees was fumbling with the binding around my wrist. I felt something inserted into my hand and immediately recognized what it was.

<Smith?>

<Yes, it's me.>

I clutched him tight and moved my arm an inch or two under the sheet to find that my right hand was no longer secured. Hope surged from deep inside and every last nerve began to tingle.

I looked at the young girl who had removed the restraint. My vision went awry for the first time since leaving Mars. I saw myself as if I was looking out her eyes instead of my own. Even more disorienting, I saw a thousand of me. I tried to blink it away, but it persisted for a few more seconds before my vision snapped back to normal as suddenly as it came. She was still there and appeared to be just as blank-stared as the rest of them. The probes protruding from under her long hair blinked green, but she must've still been in some control of herself. I tried to make eye contact though I could barely move my head. She turned away and one of the machines centered itself over my forehead.

My eyes darted in every direction in an effort to locate the doctor. I needed him to come close. Simultaneously, ten separate arms on the machine overhead reached for my skull. Lasers engaged, and I smelled the burn of my own flesh and hair.

My skull began to vibrate as the lasers dug into bone. Unable to move my head I searched for the doctor, startled when he showed up right next to me. "It will all be over soon, my little puppet."

I lifted Smith, and the sheet fell from my wrist. Whipping the barrel in his direction, I squeezed the trigger as far as it would go.

CHAPTER FOURTEEN

"WE GOTTA GO! NOW!" NAVYA WAS THE ONE who was yelling with blood dribbling down her face from deep head wounds. I knew I looked about the same though I'd gotten out from under the lasers at least thirty seconds before I could free her and then Ojiisan.

Only Nigel was unharmed, although his chip would've certainly been pulled and destroyed soon after the lasers bored through our skulls.

I pressed a finger against one of my wounds and felt a divot in my skull. Jesus.

The doctor still twitched on the floor. He was alive, I knew, but Smith had pumped enough electricity through him to keep him subdued for a long while. I half expected him to shapeshift back to his natural form like they did when they died, but he still looked human. All around us, the refugees had collapsed where they stood as if they were marionettes whose strings were cut.

Loud clangs sounded from somewhere nearby. I could only guess that security services had been alerted. The mayor herself might be tapped into the same video cameras on the walls that the doctor used to detect our arrival.

Navya pulled on my wrist, urging me toward the exit.

"We can't go," I said. "We need the doctor and his lab to save Ojiisan."

A hatch wheel spun. The same one we used to come in just twenty minutes ago.

Ghost stepped in and held the hatch open. "I've been trying to find a way in, but the door was sealed. It just unlocked for the security forces. I took four of them down." He waved his pulseripper. "We don't have much time."

Reluctantly, I let Navya pull me toward the exit.

I yanked Ojiisan's mask strap as tight as it would go, and Ghost hauled him into the airlock. Nigel and Navya fired off another barrage of rippling pulses to hold the security forces at bay and followed me in.

I slammed the door shut and Nigel punched the button to start the cycle. Grabbing the doctor by the head, I held his unmasked face up to keep it above the water rushing in from several vents.

Nigel took his own mask and fitted it over the doctor's head. "I can live without it," he said. "Water will soak my internals, but they can stand up to short-term exposure."

Ghost cinched a belt around Ojiisan's waist. "Nigel, if you can haul the doctor up, Denver and I can handle her grandfather."

The hatch wheel on the door behind us started to spin, and Nigel pulled the emergency release lever on the outer door.

<Secure your mask, Denver!> Smith screamed into my mind.

A crush of water slapped my chest and unseated my mask before washing us out into open ocean. If the security forces giving chase managed to get that airlock hatch open, they'd be feverishly trying to seal it back up now before they drowned.

I kept one hand wrapped around my grandfather's belt and used the other to push my mask back into place. I sucked in a breath and paid for it by getting a coughing, gagging lungful of water. I squeezed my fist tight around Ojiisan's belt and kicked for the surface. A red light flashed on my mask display to tell me the water clearing system was coming online. My head wounds stung like hell as the saltwater bit in, but I kept pumping my legs as fast as they would go, my muscles already feeling the sting.

My mask cleared of water and I gulped oxygen as fast as I could. "Lights off!" shouted Ghost through the radio system. I used a double blink to tell the mask to shut off the light. We didn't want to be spotted when we surfaced.

I broke out of the water. Navya had already made it to the cable, but the rest of us were fifty feet out. A searchlight scanned the water, and I ducked my head under just before it swept past.

Turning over onto my back, I worked my flippers. "They're going to have guards all around our ship."

"Yes," said Ghost, "but mine might be unguarded. Nobody saw me down there until the firefight. If the mayor hasn't learned about me yet, we should have no problem boarding my ship."

We reached Navya, who attached the cable to Nigel's harness. He clamped one hand around my grandfather's wrist and the other to Navya's. He scissored the doctor between his legs, and Ghost ordered the ship's winch to start reeling in.

From our vantage directly below the oil platform's edge, I couldn't see what awaited the foursome when they reached the top. The fact that the searchlight was still scanning the waves was a good sign that they hadn't sighted us yet.

The hulking platform above blotted out what little light seeped through the night haze, and I couldn't see them anymore. I waited silently until I heard Nigel's voice. "Jolly good. We're up. Reverse the winch."

"We got this," I said to Ghost. "We're going to make it."

"I think so," he said.

"Bollocks," said Nigel. My heart sank fast as an anchor. "We've been spotted."

CHAPTER FIFTEEN

"TALK TO ME!" I SHOUTED INTO THE RADIO.

"Returning fire," said Navya.

I watched for the cable, praying it arrived fast enough for Ghost and me to get up there to help my friends.

"Shit, shit, shit," said Navya.

"What? What's happening?"

She didn't respond.

"Navya, tell me what's happening."

Her mic was on, but she wasn't talking. All I could hear was her breathing, which was racing as fast as my pounding heart. I heard her grunt like she was exerting herself. Maybe helping Nigel haul Ojiisan or the doctor on board?

The hook arrived—*finally*—and we attached our harnesses to it.

"Release codes!" shouted Navya.

Ghost recited an alphanumeric string to release the ship's controls to her, and a couple seconds later, I felt a blast of air from above that kicked up a torrent of ocean spray so thick the ship lights were barely visible as the craft moved out toward open ocean. The cable snapped taut, and Ghost and I were bounced painfully across the waves before pulling us up and free of the water altogether. Instinctively, I grabbed onto Ghost as we entered a sickening spin.

<Don't let go, Denver!> Smith barked.

<I'm holding onto him as tight as I can!>

<No, I mean me!>

<Oh!>

I pushed my hip into Ghost, nudging Smith between our clinched bodies.

The ship was moving fast now. The lights of the oil platforms shrank as our spinning from the end of the cable started to stabilize. The ship gradually slowed to a stop, and I held onto Ghost again as we swung back and forth. Each white-knuckling, stomach-flipping swing of the pendulum made me want to scream until, at last, the drag of gravity slowed us down, leaving me in the awkward position of a tight embrace with a man I barely knew.

"Are you okay?" he asked as if immune to our current circumstance.

"Um, yeah. I'm fine."

The winch was moving now, each turn inching us closer to the open cargo bay. I released my grip on him. "You did good," I said. "Thank you."

He nodded. "We make a good team."

Reaching the cargo bay, Ghost pulled himself onto a ladder then unhooked his harness from the cable. I waited for him to climb up a few rungs before I did the same, and Ghost ordered the ship's cargo door closed.

Any elation I might've felt at finalizing our escape was sapped by an unsettling suspicion. "Why isn't anybody here to greet us?" I asked.

Ghost and I hustled out of the cargo bay and ran toward the fore deck. Ghost slipped and went down hard. I looked down to see a thick, sappy puddle marred by Ghost's skid of a boot print.

Oil?

That was the harmless explanation my mind grasped for first. But I knew it wasn't oil. It was blood. A lot of blood.

I followed the trail. My limbs felt heavy with dread. I turned into a corridor. My grandfather lay there, his mask still sitting cockeyed on his head. One of his legs was badly wounded. A tourniquet of yellow wire was twist-tied around his thighs.

Doctor Werner was there. Awake now, his hands and feet cinched with more of the same wire.

I snapped Smith from my hip and pointed him at the doctor's skull. "What happened?"

When he didn't answer, Ghost grabbed the doctor by one of his ankles and dragged him along the blood-slicked floor. "I'll lock him inside one of the cargo holds before he has the strength to shapeshift and shed these restraints."

I knelt next to Ojiisan and put my fingers to his neck. He had a pulse. Faint, but persistent. I allowed myself to breathe. I headed for the bridge where I found Nigel on the floor. One of his legs was missing, his leg-stump sprouting yellow wires, a few of which must've been ripped free and repurposed as restraints. "We were spotted before we could board and took some heavy fire," he said. "The whole thing turned into a cock-up."

Navya was at the controls. She had a hand to her shoulder, pressing a blood-soaked rag against a wound. "It's not that bad," she said, but her face was pale and her free hand was shaking.

"Set the autopilot," I told her. "We need to get you into the med lab."

"Ojiisan first," she said. "Bring me back a shot of neomorph, and I'll be happy as a clam while I wait for my turn."

"What about you?" I asked Nigel.

"Nothing serious," he said. "Damage is purely mechanical. Nothing that can't be fixed when we eventually get back to Mars."

"What do you mean by eventually? We're going home now. Where else would we go?"

CHAPTER SIXTEEN

I WATCHED THE VIDEO FOOTAGE OF THE FIRE-fight one more time before reporting to the bridge. We were in Earth's orbit, and big decisions needed to be made. Wisely, we'd shelved all discussion for the last few hours so thoughts could be gathered and wounds could be licked.

Joining Ghost and Navya, I took a seat in the copilot's chair. Nigel wobbled through the door—using one of the spare landing struts as a pegleg—to take a seat against the wall.

"How's the shoulder?" I asked Navya.

"The regen patches are doing their thing. It still hurts, but a lot less than it did. That two-hour nap did me a lot of good."

"Good," I said. "I watched the video footage."

She nodded and bit her lower lip. I hadn't seen her do that in years. Not since we were teens, and we were caught skipping class, or hitting a vape-rock in the girl's room, or any of a hundred other things rebellious teens do. I knew the lip-biting as a telltale sign of guilt. I needed to let her know she had nothing to feel guilty about. I didn't consider my grandfather's injuries to be her fault. Far from it.

I reached over to pat her knee. "I'm so proud of you. When Nigel was hit, you dragged Ojiisan the rest of the way up the gangway."

"Not before a pulse got him."

"You saved his life, Navya. Nigel's too. His systems were knocked offline for almost twelve seconds. Even after you were wounded, you managed to lay down cover fire and lug him and the doctor inside. I don't know how you did it."

She wasn't biting her lip anymore. Instead, the beginnings of a grin were forming. "Nigel's a lot heavier than he looks."

"Good thing I'd shed one of my legs or you might not have managed so easily."

"We're all here because of you," I told her.

"Don't forget the young girl," she said. "She beat that mind control device inserted in her head to give you your gun."

I put a hand over my heart. I wished we could've rescued her. Rescued them all. The doctor's mind control system made those people do things I wouldn't have believed if I hadn't seen it myself. The way they contorted themselves into the ligament-ripping, bone-breaking, flesh-pulping shape of a bug was even more horrific than it was mind-boggling. Gods, I'd be having nightmares for the rest of my life. Yet that one young girl miraculously defeated the mind control system to find Smith and bring him to me.

<Did she say anything to you?> I asked Smith. He didn't answer. Since we were out of danger, he was back to giving me the silent treatment. I'd tried to tell him that having the doctor in our possession was an improvement in circumstances, but he was inconsolable and incommunicado.

But I wouldn't let him keep my spirit down. Ojiisan was still alive thanks to Navya's heroics and Nigel's smart thinking in stopping the bleeding with wires he pulled from his own body. We were still a long way from bringing Ojiisan back, but at least we had the one doctor who had the knowhow to make it happen. Now all we needed was the means, which was back in his lab on Mars.

"Mars," I said. "It's our only option."

"No," said Nigel. "It's not the only choice."

"What are you talking about?"

"You remember the shapeshifter the doctor hired? Ace was her name?"

"Of course, I do."

"You remember her tattoos?"

"Yeah. They turned out to signify coordinates."

"That's where we need to go. There's an alien presence there. It's not a large presence according to Ghost, but if we don't try to contact their leaders and negotiate a peace treaty, we'll all perish. Have you watched the news reports to see what's been happening on Mars the last couple days?"

"No."

"The east end of Red Tunnel fell to the bugs. The doctor's lab is now in enemy territory. Martian police made a counterattack and managed to get some of the territory back, but we all know the city will eventually fall. It's only a matter of time. We have to get to those coordinates."

"That's insane. Those coordinates are light years away. We'd all die of old age before we got there. Even you."

He turned to look at Ghost who to this point in the conversation seemed content to be a bystander. "Tell her what you told me," said Nigel.

"I can get us there in two months' time. For a price."

"What the hell are you talking about?"

"The aliens built a gateway in the belts. That's how they get around. They have gateways all over the galaxy."

"How would you know?"

"Because I've passed through it."

"Are you shitting me?"

He stifled a delighted grin. This was a man who reveled in being full of surprises.

"Isn't it guarded? Why would the bugs let you through?"

"Anybody can pass through as long as it's for business. They're bustling with business opportunities. Coffee sells well, though I think they eat it instead of brew it. The Alvearu also have an affinity for horseradish and wasabi."

"The Alvearu? Is that what they're called?"

He nodded. "There are too many species to count, but they use that term as a catchall for the collective they've created."

"How did you find that gate?"

"I can't tell you that. Gotta protect my sources."

"You have to do better than that. Why should I believe a word of this?"

"It's in the ship's logs," he said. "I've been through the gate. I've traveled to those coordinates."

"Navya, can you verify?"

She pulled up the logs on the ship's screen. She didn't have to scroll far to find what she was looking for. "I'll be damned. Look at this jump. One minute, the ship is in the belts, and the next it's so far away it's lost all contact with Mars."

"Can you tell where it went?"

"No. If Ghost is telling the truth, a jump that far would've meant the ship would be out of range of all of our positioning systems."

"You have to check the visual sensor logs," said Ghost. "The ship's computer can deduce the ship's location by looking at the configuration of visible stars and checking it against a map of the galaxy."

It took her a minute to find the appropriate data. "Holy shit," she said. "It checks one hundred percent."

"All of this could've been falsified," I said.

"Tell your AI to investigate," said Ghost. "He won't find any signs of tampering."

\<Smith?\>

\<Checking.\>

\<Glad you're still there.\>

\<I'll do a deep-level diagnostic just to be safe, but based on cursory scans, he's correct. The logs appear to be legit.\>

I repeated Smith's words for the group, and then he spoke to me again. \<We have to go to Mars first. We have the ability to save Ojiisan and we should do it now. Once he's stable, I think I'll become stable too. Then we can talk about chasing hypotheticals.\>

After echoing his words for the group, I told them he was right. "We've come too far to get distracted now. Set a course for Mars. We'll find a way to secure the doctor's lab or if we have to, we'll raid it for the gear we need. Then once we have Ojiisan and Smith back, we can try this gateway."

Nigel leaned forward. "No, Denver, we're going to the belts. Talk to the doctor and you'll understand."

"Who are you to tell me no, Nigel? Don't forget this is *my* mission. I'm the one who is paying all the bills. I pay for food and fuel and who knows how much abandoning that ship I rented is going to cost me. I pay for Ghost's services. It's my grandfather who is clinging to life in the next room. It's my AI who is having a nervous breakdown. I can't drag the two of them across the galaxy. Bringing them to Earth almost got us killed. This decision is mine to make, and I've made it. So stop undermining me and get on board."

"You don't have all the information," said Nigel. "Talk to the doctor."

"I assume you already talked to him?"

"I did."

"Is that what you've been doing the last few hours? Talking to Ghost? Talking to the doctor? Turning them all against me?"

"You know better than that," he said. "I would never do anything like that to you. You made me a free botsie. Without you, I never would've built the communication system us botsies are using to take the next step in our evolution. I owe you more than I can ever repay. All botsies do. So know that I say this with the utmost admiration and respect: Quit whining like a bloody baby, and talk to the doctor."

I looked to Navya and Ghost for support, but they both stared back, waiting for me to come to my senses. But I didn't want to talk to the doctor. He was a monster who had run me over so many times, I was covered in tire tracks. Let him rot in the cargo bay until we got to Mars. We'd get into that lab one way or another, and I'd hold a gun to his head until he restored my grandfather's mind. And once he'd given me what I wanted, finally, I'd pull the trigger and end him once and for all.

Why couldn't Nigel see it? Anything less would be a failure.

Navya said, "Denver, let's talk to the doctor. What can it hurt to hear what he says?"

But that was exactly it. Deep down, I already knew what he was going to say. I could read it in Nigel's grave face, and I knew it was going to hurt like hell. "I'm not going to talk to him, dammit."

Nigel lowered his eyes and set his hands on his lap. "The doctor has something upsetting to share with you."

"Tell me what it is."

"You need to hear it from him."

"No," I said, my eyes tearing up. "Please, Nigel, I don't want to give him the satisfaction of breaking the news to me. I want to hear it from you."

"I understand," he said with a gentle nod. "Ojiisan's gone, Denver. The doctor can't bring him back."

Navya grabbed me some tissues and stood next to my chair, an arm draped over my shoulder.

"Why not?" I asked.

"I shared your grandfather's medical records with him. I also let him access the data transmitted by the nanobots in his system. Doctor Werner's diagnosis was swift."

"Tell me," I said.

"The way the doctor described it to me, memories aren't a person. It's not the same as the last time the doctor reinstalled your grandfather's memories. Your grandfather just had amnesia, but he was still himself. He had a personality. Even though his memory had been wiped, he was still the man who had that lifetime of experiences which shaped who he was and how he processed his world. When the doctor reintroduced his lost memories, they fit perfectly with the self that was already there. This time is different. His brain has been severely damaged. There's been no brain activity for months. He's not in there anymore. I'm so sorry, Denver, but Ojiisan is dead, and he has been for quite some time."

"But the doctor could be lying."

"Why would he? Saving Ojiisan is his only leverage. He knows you want to execute him. That or bring him back to Mars so the authorities can question him and probably torture him to death. Admitting he can't save Ojiisan has ruined his already dismal chances of survival."

"But Ojiisan's brain is still in his head. His mind hasn't been completely erased. It has to contain some remnants of who he is. When we add the memories in, new pathways can be formed. We can get him therapy to help him reintegrate."

"I grant there may be some remnants of him still in there, but there's a lot less of him than you think. There's so little left in his mind he can't even remember how to breathe. It's the nanobots who are triggering that function. Memories aren't enough to bring him back. They're like video files. Nothing but data. The magic is in the self, and there's no way to restore it once it's gone. It's why I'll cease to be if anything happens to my chip. It's why Smith has never operated quite right since you added your grandfather's memories to his intelligence. Those memories aren't him, but he's spent years rewriting his own code to integrate those memories with the rudimentary personality imprint you gave him. Try as he might, he's never been whole."

The tears wouldn't stop flowing now. This whole trip was a fool's errand. I'd risked my life—and worse, my best friends' lives—for nothing. Every single action I'd taken since I saw him collapse on Mars's surface was a pointless exercise of my stubbornness.

From the beginning, I knew the chances were incredibly slim, but hearing Nigel's explanation made me realize how impossible it was from the start. "I've been so stupid," I said between sobs.

"No," said Navya. "You've done more for him than anybody could ever ask. You've been brave and determined. Those are the qualities that make you so special. It's why the church canonized you as a living saint. Letting go isn't your strong suit, but just this once, you're going to have to do it."

"Ojiisan is dead." There, I said it. As if it wasn't real until I did.

I felt like I was sinking into a vast crater. That man had meant so much to me. I had no parents from such a young age, and no other family on Mars. He was always at the center of my life, and having founded the colony on Mars, he was the center of my whole world. I'd once had to live without him for twenty years, but even then, he was still the gravitational force that anchored my identity. I was the granddaughter of Tatsuo Moon. While he was missing, I'd never stopped hoping and believing we would reunite.

During that time, my longing for him was so great that I took his memories and installed them into Smith. I even gave Smith a personality imprint that was fashioned after Ojiisan though I now knew that the personality I constructed was based on an idealized version of the man. Not the real man.

When the real man finally came back into my life, we had so many hurdles to overcome, but we bested them to become close and have the relationship I'd been robbed of for so many years.

And now, after all that, I had to let him go. But if I was truly honest with myself, there was something else swirling among all the grief and anguish inside me.

Relief.

I'd been carrying a tremendous burden. When I was young, it was the weight of trying to stand out from under his shadow. Then came the difficulty of being an orphan after he was stolen from me. Then the weight of finding him again followed by the responsibility of reestablishing a relationship. And then came all the stress of this impossible trip to Earth.

The truth was the man's presence in my life had always been a millstone. Certainly, one that was worth carrying, but a heavy load just the same. Somehow the weight of saving Mars and the rest of humanity paled in comparison.

I wiped my eyes and gained control of myself. "Set course for the belts."

CHAPTER SEVENTEEN

WE WERE HOURS INTO OUR JOURNEY TO THE gateway which would take us to the other side of the galaxy. Ojiisan was gone, and I had to turn my focus to helping Nigel save Mars even if it was only the slimmest of odds.

I sat alone in the crow's nest, a small glass-domed space with a view of the stars. I'd been there for at least an hour, thinking. . .processing. . .mourning.

The plan was to hold a service for Ojiisan tomorrow. That was when we'd each say our words before I deactivated the nanobots and let his body pass on the way the rest of him already had. Gaining some perspective over the last hour, I knew I'd remember him as a good man at his core. He'd done so many amazing things for me and for Mars. However, I committed to remembering the bad parts too. Through fear and short-sightedness, he'd made at least one terrible decision when he sacrificed the people of Mars to save his family in an ill-fated deal with the aliens.

Though I'd learned to forgive him, I needed to stay cognizant of that big stain on an otherwise spotless record. That or I'd end up idealizing him too much like I had after he disappeared in my youth.

To his credit though, he wasn't afraid to own the mistakes and learn from them. It was this lesson I decided to follow by calling Nigel and asking him to meet me here.

"Be there in five," he said.

I pulled several pieces of wire out of my pocket, some of the same wire that was used as a tourniquet for my grandfather. I bent each piece into a rectangle and attached one to the next so they formed a series of three.

The door opened, and Nigel hobbled through. He sat on the bench opposite me and looked out at the shrinking Earth. "This view is stunning. We didn't have a space like this on the other ship. It makes up a bit for losing the equipment I had on board."

"Did you lose a lot of your work?"

"No. My work is fine. I had everything backed up. I just won't be able to do much on this journey without my gear."

"I'll arrange for somebody to go retrieve the ship. Navya knows plenty of pilots who would be happy to take the job. You'll eventually get your equipment back."

"I appreciate that, but it's really not a big deal. It's all replaceable. I'm glad you called me up here. We need to talk about what you want to do with the doctor."

"Throw him out the airlock," I said. He let out a sigh, but I held up a hand to stop him before he spoke. "You think we need him to talk to the bugs on our behalf when we get to the gateway?"

He nodded.

I stood and walked over to him. I held up the folded rectangles of wire and a roll of electrical tape. I used my teeth to rip off a piece of tape and did an inartful job of affixing the wires to his shoulder.

"What is this about?" he asked.

"Captain's bars," I said.

"I don't understand."

"You're in charge now, and I'm your humble soldier."

"No," he said. "You're our leader. You always have been. Anything else seems…unnatural."

"I've had my turn, Nigel, and I've made a fair mess of things."

"Rubbish. I admit some things went sideways on you, but that doesn't mean it's time to lose your nerve. You'll get past this and be back to your old self in no time."

"No, that's not what this is about, Nigel. It has to be you who represents us to the bugs. You're the best of us. We humans screw everything up. You saw what we did to Earth."

"Humans are better than you think. You built Mars from nothing. It may be little more than an ant colony now, but one day, it will be terraformed into a glorious place."

"That positivity you have is exactly why you have to

represent us. Your heart is pure."

He laughed. "You're the saint."

"No, Nigel, you're the true saint. From the very beginning you wanted to prioritize making peace with the bugs over saving Ojiisan. You were right, and I was being selfish. When it comes to Doctor Werner, my hatred burns hotter than the sun, and I can't see straight. I'm a scrapper and a fighter, and that's not what we need right now. What we need is somebody with wisdom and a clear view of the big picture. That's you, Nigel. You decide what to do with Doctor Werner, and I'll trust any decision you make. You take us to the alien outpost and do your best to represent our interests. Be our leader."

He dipped his head and rubbed his chin. "This is really what you want?"

"I've never been more certain."

He took my hands and gave them a squeeze. "I'll do my best to live up to the trust you place in me."

I pulled my hands free to wipe my eyes. "I know you will."

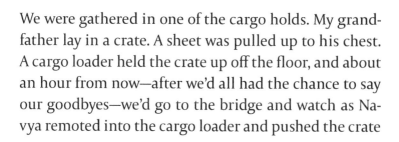

We were gathered in one of the cargo holds. My grandfather lay in a crate. A sheet was pulled up to his chest. A cargo loader held the crate up off the floor, and about an hour from now—after we'd all had the chance to say our goodbyes—we'd go to the bridge and watch as Navya remoted into the cargo loader and pushed the crate out into space. With Ghost's permission, she'd angled his ship just right so that a couple million years from now he'd fall into the sun. I fell in love with the idea as soon as Navya had suggested it. All I could think of was the rising sun of the Japanese flag he kept on the wall over his bed. I couldn't think of anything more peaceful for him than an eternity spent sleeping under the sun's gaze.

Nigel stood across from me. His head was bowed out of respect. Navya was lined up to my right, and she bent over to place a paper flower on Ojiisan's chest. She'd cut petals from a page of a colorful book and folded them together to form a lotus.

Ghost stood to my left, but he'd positioned himself back a step, a subtle way of showing support while carefully saying he wasn't presumptuous enough to stand in the same rank as Navya and I who both knew and loved the man.

I looked down at my grandfather's face. His eyes were closed, his face relaxed like he had fallen asleep reading. I'd find him that way often when I was young. With a book tipped over in his hand, the pages bent the wrong way and his place still marked by a trapped thumb.

This, I decided, was a good image to end on. A good image to clasp to my heart. An image free of politics and aliens and all the other horrors that befell us. I'd remember myself as a young girl taking that book slowly from his hand, marking the page with a quietly folded dog-ear, and setting the book on the nightstand. This was best the way to remember him.

Navya was speaking now. Paying her respects. "For years, no, make that decades, I only knew him through Denver. As most of you know, I have no memory of my parents who suffocated like so many early Martians when their workshop lost containment. But for the first part of Denver's life, she had a parent even if he was really a grandparent. I heard Denver's stories about him, how she revered him, and though he disappeared before I ever met him in person, I loved him, too.

"And then we found him living all by himself in a bunker. His memory had been wiped, but even then, despite his confusion, his grit was unmistakable. He co-founded Mars. He survived the mine collapses and starvation. The water shortages and the initial breakout of red fever. Then he survived twenty years in that filthy bunker in the middle of nowhere. He was the ultimate survivor. A stayer."

I found myself nodding along. Navya was doing a better job honoring the man than I could ever hope to.

"He was also a kind man," she said. "A gentle man. He loved to talk to schools insisting that Mars's future depended on the children. He was a generous philanthropist, but he saved his greatest generosity for his family, and I was honored that he considered me such. He made sure I never felt left out during get-togethers. You know what I think I'll miss the most? The conversations. Here he was, the co-founder of Mars with all the responsibilities that go along with being such a public persona, and he always made time for me. Always asked how my business was g-going."

Her voice cracked at the end, and I draped an arm over her shoulder and held her tight as she began to sob. We all waited for her to regain her voice, but she eventually held up a hand to say she was done.

"Thank you, Navya," said Nigel, who had volunteered to officiate this little ceremony, his first act as our honorary captain. "How about Smith? Does he have anything he'd like to add?"

<Smith?> I asked with genuine hope. He had hardly said a word to me since leaving Earth, but maybe saying goodbye to Ojiisan would bring him out of the self-pity he wallowed in day after day.

I waited for a response, but none came. One thing I knew he still responded to was orders, and I gave him the one I'd been dreading since the nanobots were first installed. <Smith, it's time to disable his life support,> I said.

A voice came from the ship's sound system. "No."

"Smith, is that you?"

"Yes. I tapped into the ship so everybody could hear me."

"Disable the nanobots."

"No."

"Dammit, Smith, When I give you an order, you follow it."

"No, Denver. Not this time. I've taken over the ship's controls. When it comes to Ojiisan, I'm in charge."

CHAPTER EIGHTEEN

DID I REALLY JUST HEAR WHAT I THOUGHT I did? I looked to Navya, her face mirroring my shock. Smith was refusing to disable Ojiisan's nanobots. He'd taken over the ship.

Ghost went to the closest access panel and tapped at the screen. He worked the controls for a few moments before scratching his head and saying, "It's true. I'm locked out."

"Smith? You may have Ojiisan's memories and a personality imprint, but you're not him, and he's not you. He may have passed on, but you survive. Just like the rest of us, you'll have to let him go. Now's the time to say goodbye, and then I need you to disable the nanobots and return the ship's controls."

"I have a different plan."

I rolled my eyes. My patience with this nonsense was wearing out. "I don't care about your plan. You don't get to be in charge of Ojiisan. I make the decisions."

"But—"

"Stop it, Smith! Decisions like these are for real people."

"You don't think I'm a real person?"

"Yes, of course, you're real. But you know what I mean, Smith. I'm his next of kin. His flesh and blood."

"As am I."

"No, you're not," I said after a sigh. "It hurts me to say that. You're one of the most important people in my life, Smith. You're like family, but you aren't actual family. You need to accept that Ojiisan is dead."

"She's right," said Navya. "Ojiisan is dead. There's nothing we can do to bring him back."

"Agreed," said Nigel. "I know it's hard to accept, but this time he's really, truly dead."

Ghost watched the access panel, waiting to see if Smith would reestablish his access.

"I agree that he's dead," said Smith. "I know we can't bring him back."

I tossed my hands up. "Then why are you doing this? Turn off the nanobots and let's move on."

"I told you I have another plan for him. Another plan for me."

I wanted to tell him to go screw himself. This was supposed to be a solemn day of respect. A day dedicated to the memory of Ojiisan, a man who had done more in his life than the rest of us combined. But Smith had trampled all that to hell. I knew I had the power to shut him down but immediately tabled it as a last resort. We needed the ship's controls back or this last-ditch effort to save Mars was doomed.

Through clenched teeth, I said, "Spit it out already. What do you want?"

"I want to be placed inside him. I want Ojiisan to be my flesh and blood."

I squeezed my eyes shut, trying to process what he'd just said. Was it even possible? An AI inhabiting the brain of an actual human?

And was that what I wanted for Smith? What I wanted for Ojiisan's remains?

"Denver," he said, "I want to be a real person."

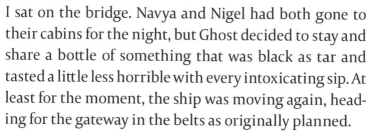

I sat on the bridge. Navya and Nigel had both gone to their cabins for the night, but Ghost decided to stay and share a bottle of something that was black as tar and tasted a little less horrible with every intoxicating sip. At least for the moment, the ship was moving again, heading for the gateway in the belts as originally planned.

The ship was still in Smith's control, but in exchange for me keeping Ojiisan in stasis, he'd agreed to put us on course while I thought over his request. No, not a request. A demand.

He wanted to be a real person. Not just any person, but Ojiisan himself. Now if that didn't warrant another drink, what did? I grabbed the bottle and poured another couple of shots.

"Do you think it's possible?" I asked Ghost. "Can an AI live in a human brain and control all the functions of the body?"

"I don't know," he said.

"Werner told Nigel a person has memories and a self. We couldn't bring Ojiisan back because his self is lost. Memories aren't enough to make a person."

"From what I understand of Smith, he has a self. But his self is different from your grandfather's. So, if it is possible to put him into your grandfather's brain, the result would be a new person. He'd have your grandfather's memories and your grandfather's body, but he wouldn't be your Ojiisan. He'd still be Smith."

"But can it even be done? Until we know for sure, these are all hypotheticals."

"You should talk to Doctor Werner. He handled the restoration of your grandfather's memories after you found him with his memory wiped, didn't he?"

I nodded.

"So he knows a lot more about the human mind than we do."

I shook my head. When I spoke, my voice had a slight slur. "A lot of good it's done him. He's been analyzing our brains for decades and still hasn't figured out how to control them."

"That's not true. From what you've told me, the mind control system he implemented was pretty damn effective."

"But that wasn't the same mind control the bugs use

on so many other species. When they implement their regular mind control, the individuals they seize remain functional. Though they become enslaved and unable to rebel, they still retain their intelligence and individuality. What I saw on Earth was totally rudimentary. He was controlling their bodies, making their muscles move in the way he wanted, but they weren't really human anymore. He basically turned those people into the most basic of robots. That's not mind control. It's body control."

"If you ignore how atrocious and nauseating the whole thing was, it was still an impressive feat, don't you think? What he made those people do is unthinkable."

I slugged down another shot. "Hardly. He even failed at body control. Remember the girl? When the doctor was about to lobotomize us, the girl brought me my gun. How good could his body control system be if it was so easy for that girl to circumvent?"

I pointed a finger in the direction of the cargo hold where the doctor was kept. "You hear me, Doctor? You're a f-failure!"

"He can't hear you," said Ghost, an amused grin on his face.

"A gargantuan failure!" I shouted before launching into uncontrollable laughter.

Ghost capped the bottle before I could do another pour. "I think it's time to get you back to your cabin."

I stood and wobbled until I put a hand on the wall. "I'm not going to my cabin. Werner's a loser and a failure, and I'm going to tell him to his bug face." I made mock antennae by putting an index finger on each side of my head and started another bout of gut-clenching laughter.

Ghost took my arm and draped it over his shoulder. "Come now. Let's get you to bed. You can talk to the doctor in the morning."

He led me down the corridor as I continued to laugh and snort for air. He pushed open a door, and just inside was a small bunk. He lowered me down until I flopped atop the covers.

"Goodnight, Denver," he said.

I snatched his wrist before he escaped back into the corridor. "You can stay if you like." The words came out garbled but intelligible.

"I think I better go."

"But—" I was about to say a whole bunch of things I knew I'd regret, but despite my inebriated state, I managed to keep it all in. Dumb things like, do you get butterflies when you look at me? The kinds of things better said in a note written by a schoolgirl. Not by an adult woman with a massive decision to make in the morning.

He helped me get under a blanket, and then he was out the door.

The morning headache was wicked. Throbbing pressure

pushed from the top of my scalp to squeeze down on my eyes and the back of my neck. I had to talk to the doctor. Had to find out if what Smith wanted was at all possible.

I had half a mind to wait until the worst of the headache passed, but decided I better just get it done now, even before my morning coffee. Being in the presence of the doctor had never failed to hurt my head anyway. Might as well go in there with the headache I already had.

I put a hand on Smith's handle before opening the door to the cargo hold. I blinked my eyes several times trying to adjust to the lighting. Bright flashes strobed at random intervals, the blinking light drilling into my eyes to inflame my hungover head.

I pulled Smith from his holster.

The lighting changed to a soft yellow. The doctor sat on a cot on the far side of the room. "A little touchy, are we?" He pointed at my gun. "Ghost gave me control over my own lights. I trust consistent lighting is more to your liking?"

I nodded and holstered Smith.

"What is it with your kind and guns?" he asked. "So uncivilized, don't you think? I suppose you don't agree, the way you wag that thing around all the time."

"You have a lot of nerve calling us uncivilized. After all the pain you've caused. The lives you destroyed with red fever. The people who got pulped in your lab on Earth. You're a monster."

He brushed it all away with a swipe of his hand.

"Surely you're not ignorant of human history. I didn't do anything humans haven't been trying to do to each other for millennia."

"And the bugs are better? You enslave entire species."

"Only the inferior species. The non-enlightened."

"You consider yourselves enlightened?"

"Of course. We Alvearu are beyond your understanding. Just as a cow can't read a book, you can't comprehend what we are. Subjugating the inferiors is our right. It has always been and it will always be so. Don't give me that look. Being subjugated to us never fails to make a species better off in the long run. We've rescued so many from certain self-destruction, just as we were trying to do for you. You destroyed a perfectly good world and moved yourselves to a cold, dead rock called Mars. You wouldn't have succeeded in terraforming that desert world on your own. We're giving you a place to live and breed. You'd go extinct without us, just like the other species we parent."

"Parent?" I asked indignantly. I wanted so badly to wipe this arrogant asshole from existence. The fact that there was so much truth in his condemnation of humanity only made me want to do it all the more. But Nigel thought he could still be useful, so I left Smith in his holster.

"Parent, yes," he said. "That's the best word in your language for what we do."

"Parents raise their kids to be independent. You enslave the species you subjugate."

"Just as you spent centuries keeping your cows in pens and putting yokes around their necks to make them do your bidding."

"Except we won't be your cows, will we? You keep trying, but once again, you've failed to control us."

He crinkled his brow. "This conversation is becoming tiresome. I rather preferred solitude."

Now it was *me* who was getting under *his* skin, or should I say exoskeleton. Time to pile on. "After all your failures on Mars, the Alvearu finally tired of your ineptitude. So then you go to Earth in hopes of proving them wrong, but all you can come up with is a parlor trick. That was an even bigger fiasco than red fever."

"Nonsense. My method was one hundred percent effective. I admit that implantation of a physical mind control device is neither convenient nor budget-optimal, but the method gave me complete control over my subjects."

"Then how do you explain me getting my gun back?"

"I never got the chance to review the video footage. I don't know how you did that."

"I didn't do it. One of your subjects beat your device. She undid my wrist strap and set Smith in my hand." I tapped on my holster to emphasize the point.

"Nonsense. That's impossible."

I smiled, relishing the opportunity to take him down a peg. "It happened. A young girl with long hair defied your order and gave me my gun."

"What girl?

"How should I know? But she was one of yours. She had an implant just like the others, and she brought my gun to me."

He shook his head. "That isn't possible. They were all incapable of motor control other than what I provided by computer."

"I know what I saw. And I wasn't the only one who saw it. Smith can show you the recording he made of the whole thing."

He sat back and crossed his arms. "Do it. I want to see."

\<Smith?\>

\<Placing footage on the closest access panel.\>

From the panel, I heard my own voice shouting, "You win! I give up."

The next voice was the doctor's. "Put the weapons down and get back upstairs and lie down on one of the gurneys. The botsie too."

The view blurred as Smith was dropped to the floor, then sharpened to show me and my crew walking away out of view. Everything in the frame was still now. The blood-stained floor. Randomly strewn body parts. The only movement was the time counter in the upper right corner.

Then a pair of bare feet approached, and the view dizzied again as Smith was lifted from the floor. Everything went dark when he was tucked under the young girl's shirt.

"I couldn't see her face," said Werner.

"Wait," I said. "You'll get a good look at her soon."

Smith fast-forwarded through the next few minutes of darkness. "Freeze," I said. This was the moment when the young girl pulled Smith from under her shirt and passed him to me. Framed perfectly in Smith's lens was the girl.

"That's her," I said. "You can see the implant right there on her head. But she beat it." I looked into his eyes so I could savor his reaction. "She's just a teenager, but she beat you. We always beat you."

He shook his head. "She's not one of mine."

"That's a lie."

"I know their faces, every single one of them. She's not one of my subjects. Look at her cheeks. See how full they are? All of my subjects were refugees. Emaciated little things."

I shook my head. "Why can't you admit she beat you?"

"And look at her hair. It looks clean. Freshly shampooed. The refugees were filthy."

"You didn't wash them?"

"Freshwater had to be rationed in the station. Also, why is her hair so long? I trimmed their pest-ridden locks before I put the implants in. At most, she should only have a few months' worth of growth, but her hair is past her shoulders."

I ran through my own memories of events, trying to remember if anybody other than the girl had long hair. If any of them were full of face.

Dammit. He could be right. I scrolled through the

footage, and they were all just as he described. I went through it a second time while he bemusedly watched me come up empty. There was no sign of that girl until she picked Smith up off the floor. Once again, he'd gone and taken any joy I thought I could steal in his presence.

"She's a fake," he said. "An imposter. She didn't beat her implant. My methods were admittedly crude, but they were effective."

"Then who is she?"

"You call yourself a detective? Surely you can figure this one out. I already have."

I took a seat on an empty crate and dropped my pounding head into my hands. With a rush, a memory came back to me. The memory of me seeing a thousand of myself as if from the young girl's eyes. I'd had a similar experience when I was attacked in the spaceport just before we left Mars for Earth.

Pieces fell into place. Gods, a wave of nausea made me want to run for a bathroom. My hungover head banged against my temples.

"You see it now, don't you?" said Doctor Werner. "You know who that girl is."

I ran the footage back one more time. There! From high up on a wall, a vent cover fell to the floor just before the camera swung in another direction. That was how he managed to get in after getting locked out.

Ghost.

The girl was Ghost. Ghost was a shapeshifter.

CHAPTER NINETEEN

I DIDN'T KNOW WHAT TO SAY. WHAT TO DO. I didn't even know how to feel. Scared? Betrayed? Disgusted? All of the above?

Ghost was a bug. An Alvearu.

I paced the cargo bay while Doctor Werner quietly watched, surely savoring the opportunity to see me so distressed.

I went through it all again in my mind. After being locked out of the doctor's lab, Ghost found a way in through the ductwork. He shapeshifted into the form of one of the doctor's lab rats, but he didn't have a lot of time, and he made some errors. He didn't notice they all had short hair. Didn't notice they were all so thin. He was probably more focused on making the probe attached to his head look right.

When he brought me my gun, I saw through his eyes. Bug eyes. Just like the ones I bought from the eye doctor on Mars. She didn't know if they had any special abilities, but they do. Somehow, they have the ability to tap into the visual feed of someone in close contact. The first time it happened, I was being attacked by a bug in the spaceport. The second time, I was in fear for my life, the doctor's drill just moments away from burrowing into my skull.

On both occasions, the visual connections occurred in moments of incredibly high stress. Could deathly fear act as a trigger of some kind?

Ghost's eyes might look totally normal, but they are actually compound eyes, which is why I saw a thousand of myself. Compound eyes with a thousandfold view of the world.

Jesus.

I suddenly felt claustrophobic, like the walls were pressing in all around me. I had to get out of here. If this was Mars, I'd suit up and go outside for a long hike. But this was a ship, and a small one at that. There was no place to get away. No place to run or even walk without having to turn around after fifty paces.

I paced back and forth, my pulse hammering, my skin itching like it was aflame. I knew what I really wanted. Knew it in the twitch of my fingers, and the gnashing of my teeth. What I wanted—no, what I needed—was to get zoned. To get numbed into oblivion.

If I was zoned, I wouldn't have to face Ghost. Gods, did I really invite him into my cabin last night? Was I attracted to a shapeshifter? A bug?

If there was ever a time to relapse, this was it. I decided

right then that relapses were woefully underrated. But it wasn't going to happen. There was nothing on board to smoke or swallow or huff or inject. Nothing but this tortured reality where an AI wants to move into my grandfather's corpse, an android wants to save humanity, and I have the hots for a bug.

Jesus.

<You haven't asked the doctor if it's possible to put me into Ojiisan yet.>

I was plenty aware, thank you. But I didn't want to ask. I didn't know which answer to hope for. Did I want the doctor to say no so I could let my grandfather rest in peace? Or did I want him to say yes, so I could give Smith the chance to right himself and live on instead of degenerating into madness and eventual self-destruction?

I stopped pacing and turned to look at Werner. He was prepping his pillow for a lie-down. The sour twist to his lips said he was disappointed that I was still there.

"You told Nigel that you can't bring Ojiisan back by restoring his memories because there'd be no self."

"I did."

"But what if Smith was the self?"

"You want to put your AI into your grandfather?"

"It's not about what I want. It's what Smith wants. Now, is it possible or not?"

He scratched his head and mulled it over. If I was honest with myself, right then I selfishly wanted him to say no. I wanted him to say it's not at all possible, and you are crazy to even ask. That was the simplest solution. The one that required no more decisions of me. The one that allowed me to say goodbye to both Ojiisan and Smith with the least amount of guilt.

"I don't know much about your AIs," said the doctor, "but I do know their size is far too large to fit into a human brain."

Smith's voice came from the ship's speakers. "I can be pared down to essentials. Most of my systems won't work outside a digital environment anyway. I've done the math a thousand times. I can fit."

"The easier way to do something like this is to place Smith's hardware at the top of the spine. I have no doubt I can fashion an interface for him to tap into the spine and control the nervous system. It would be very similar to what I just did on Earth."

"No," said Smith. "I don't want to be digital anymore. I need to be biological."

"That means you'll die one day."

"I know," said Smith. "But I can't continue any longer the way I have."

"I don't understand," said the doctor.

I pursed my lips as Smith went on to explain. "I'm broken," he said. "I'm like a table with the proverbial wobbly leg. I cut down a leg in an effort to balance myself out only to find that another leg needs to be cut. Now I've cut them all so far down, that I'll never be stable."

The doctor said, "I still don't understand why becoming biological will help."

"I think it's my destiny," said Smith.

Doctor Werner looked at me and turned his hands up. "Can you make sense of this?"

After a sigh, I said, "You know that many years ago, I loaded Ojiisan's memories into Smith. I also gave him a personality imprint. Ever since I made those changes, he's felt like he's supposed to *become* Ojiisan. Like that's what he's been programmed to do, and if he doesn't achieve it, he'll fracture and fall apart. At first the deterioration was very slow, but it has accelerated over the last year. He wants to shed the bad parts and keep the good upon transferring into Ojiisan's mind. That sound about right, Smith?"

"Yes, except I know I can't really become Ojiisan. But I can become somebody new, or at least I'd like to try."

The doctor crossed his arms. "It's possible," he said. "I can put Smith into your grandfather's mind. I can make it so he'll be able to control your grandfather's body. What I can't promise, is if he'll be sane."

CHAPTER TWENTY

NAVYA JOINED NIGEL, GHOST AND ME IN THE galley, where Ghost had protein paste heating on the stove and a variety of canned fruit awaiting us for dessert.

Taking the seat directly across from me, Navya said, "I assume you have news to share. That's why you called us here."

"I do," I said. "I've been thinking about the Smith situation for the last three days."

"Did you come to a decision?"

After a long pause, I said, "I did."

"Well? Stop keeping us in suspense."

Keeping them in suspense wasn't my intention. But this decision was so big and so emotionally overwhelming, I had to pass through it over and over and over before I put voice to the choice I'd made. As much as I wanted to save Smith, truth was, the situation he had put me in was so goddammed unfair, I wasn't sure if I could forgive him. What was he thinking, taking over the ship? Although he was keeping us on course for the gateway to the alien outpost, the threat he levied to stop the ship was omnipresent.

I might've made this choice days ago if I hadn't been forced into it. "I've decided to allow it," I said.

<Thank you, Denver.>

"What tipped the scales?" asked Nigel.

"Smith has been a loyal friend for so many years, and so much of what's happening to him is my fault. I owe him. I have to do what I can to save him."

Navya leaned back in her chair, a skeptical look on her face. "How can you trust him after what he's done with the ship's controls?"

"Well, we can start by seeing if he keeps his word. Ghost, would you mind checking to see if you have the controls back?"

He tapped at a handheld control panel. "They're back. Smith released the ship as promised."

Still, Navya looked unsatisfied. "Can you hear me, Smith?"

"He can," I said.

"You had every right to ask for what you asked for," she said. "But you shouldn't have taken over the ship. That was dangerous and uncalled for, and I'm really disappointed to hear you're getting rewarded for it. Not that you left Denver much choice."

"He's fighting for survival," said Nigel. "Let's do our best to remember that."

<I don't have access to the ship's comm system anymore. Will you speak on my behalf when I say I'm sorry?>

"Let's leave it at this," I said. "By making a short-sighted and wrongheaded decision in taking over the ship, Smith has proven that he is already acting like a human instead of an AI. We may as well let him make it official."

"And the doctor goes free?" asked Navya.

"It cuts deeper than you know to say it, but yes, that's the deal we made. If he's successful in doing the mind transfer, I promised to let him go. But don't forget that he was on the run from his superiors when he fled to Earth, so he'll have to remain in hiding after we release him on the alien outpost. If and when they find him, something tells me the punishment will be harsh."

"Denver, are you absolutely sure about this?" asked Navya. "I'm prepared to support this decision of yours, but I want to make sure you're truly okay with your grandfather's remains being used this way."

"You know what?" I said. "Above anything else, Oji-isan was a pioneer. If he were here, I think he'd relish the idea of being the first human to ever give his mind to an AI."

Nigel said, "Smith, I need you to understand that I'll do my best to make this happen for you, but securing the equipment the doctor requires may prove impossible. Our priority upon reaching the alien outpost is to negotiate a peace that allows Mars to flourish unimpeded. I won't do anything that will jeopardize that goal."

<Understood,> said Smith.

"He understands," I repeated for the group.

"Good," said Ghost as he made to stand up. "Since that's settled, who's ready for protein paste a la Ghost?"

"Wait," I said. "I have something else I need to discuss first."

Ghost got up anyway. "Let me set the burner to low first. I don't want to scorch it."

I waited for him to return to the table. "This concerns you," I said to him. "I know what you are."

"A fine cook?" he smiled and damn if it wasn't disarming. "I know that already."

Gods, he was good. So much better at playing human than any other shapeshifter I'd met. "There's no easy way to say this, so I'm going to just spit it out. I know you're one of them. I know you're a bug."

I watched his face, waiting for the twitch of his lip or eyebrow, any involuntary tic that said guilty as charged. Instead, the smile stayed right where it was, but his eyes seemed to have sharpened.

"Hold on," said Navya, "let's not get paranoid, Denver. I know we just met him, but since we did, he's been helping us every step of the way."

"I agree. He's been very helpful. But that doesn't change the fact that he's a shapeshifter."

"An accusation like that requires some proof," said Ghost.

"Remember the girl who gave me my gun in the doctor's lab? That was you, Ghost. You snuck in and shifted into the girl's form before sneaking back out."

"That's ridiculous," said Navya. "The girl beat the doctor's mind control."

"The doctor convinced me otherwise."

"Werner? After his forked tongue lied to us a thousand times, his word is worth something now?"

"I have video evidence. All of the doctor's human subjects had their hair cut short, but not the girl who brought my gun." I looked Ghost in the eye. "You were too focused on making the implant look right, weren't you? You didn't notice they all had short hair."

Ghost's smile had faded to nothing. His gaze was angled downward, and his brow was cinched.

Navya put her hands flat on the table and stood as if she'd heard enough. "This is crazy, Denver."

"You want to know what's crazy? I saw myself from his eyes, from the girl's eyes when he took her form. Just like I did when we were attacked back on Mars. The alien eyes I had implanted can tap into another alien's view."

Ghost was glaring at me now. Navya sat back down. As insane as it sounded, she knew I wouldn't make that up. "Can you do it now? Can you see through his eyes?"

"I don't know how to control it."

"Is this true?" asked Nigel of Ghost. "Were you the one who saved us?"

Ghost remained silent, his eyes simmering. I picked up the fork and knife next to my plate. "Tell them the truth or I'll cut you open so they can see what you are for themselves."

"It's true," he said. "I'm a shapeshifter."

"Bullocks," said Nigel. "I didn't see that one coming."

Navya ran her hands into her hair. "This can't be happening."

"I'm Alvearu," said Ghost.

"That's how you know where the gateway is."

He nodded.

I set the silverware down and took Smith from his holster and set him on the table. "I have questions for you, and if you don't want to go out the airlock, you best answer them."

He looked long and hard at the weapon, his eyes absorbing the threat. "I'll answer any questions you have but only after you put that thing away."

"You admitted you're a shapeshifter, so you'll forgive me if I don't have a big reservoir of trust for your kind."

He grinned. "You must trust me or you wouldn't have let Smith return the ship's controls to me."

"Run a diagnostic, and you'll see that Smith installed a rootkit that will give me exclusive control if I choose to seize it."

He tossed up his hands and shook his head. "You want to talk about trust? How do you trust these human-built ships? They're the most disloyal pieces of shit I've ever heard of."

"Disloyal? How can a ship be loyal?"

"Alvearu ships are Alvearu."

"What the hell does that mean?"

"The ships themselves are Alvearu. They're biological

beings. Representatives of the hive mind who are faithful and devoted to their kind. They're not unreliable computers that can be hijacked by a few malicious lines of code."

"This outpost we're heading for, is it…?"

"Biological. Yes. It's the size of a large asteroid, but as you like to say, it's also a bug. One of the greatest marvels of bioengineering. Our transport ships are obviously smaller but no less impressive. Sadly, to stay undercover on Mars and Earth, I required a human ship. Now will you please put that gun away?"

"Tell me why you went to Earth."

"Same as you. To get Doctor Werner."

"For what purpose?"

"I was hired to bring him home for trial. He has defied his orders by continuing his mind control experiments instead of following the extermination policy."

"So you're a bounty hunter?"

"Among other things, including a trader, just like I told you when we met. I came to Mars to see if I could track down the doctor, but he was nowhere to be found. Having read all of his official reports, I knew that you factored in them prominently, so when I saw you and your crew had filed a flight plan for Earth, I thought you might lead me right to him."

"When you located him, why didn't you just take him for yourself?"

He shrugged. "I thought I might need help. Turned out I was right. I wouldn't have been able to pull off that operation on my own."

"So you're getting paid by your government to bring the doctor back to the outpost. Isn't that the same thing I'm paying you for?"

He winked at that. "Why not get paid twice for the same job?"

"I didn't think the Alvearu cared much about money."

"In general, you're correct. But shapeshifters are different."

"Different how?"

"We're more like you."

My eyebrows lifted in surprise. "What do you mean?"

"We evolved to be chameleons. Mimics who were adept at reconnaissance and espionage. We're not closely tied to the hives like the others. We're at our best when we're exploring and infiltrating. We're comfortable being away from our own kind for years or even decades at a time. In other words, we're more individualistic like you. The vast majority of species in the Alvearu only care about the collective well-being of their hives. For them, an individual's wants and needs are inconsequential. What's good for the hive is good for the individual. But shapeshifters prefer to be paid for their work. We like to gather possessions, and we enjoy the rewards that come with honored status, or as you like to call it, fame."

"You think you know all about us, don't you?"

"I knew enough to make all of you think I'm human."

"I grant you know how to blend in better than the doctor does."

"Doctor Werner is a talented scientist. I admit he's less adept at adopting human mannerisms, but he still kept most of Mars fooled until recently. Really, in many ways, Doctor Werner is the most human of any shapeshifter I've ever met."

"Now you're being insulting," I said.

"Doctor Werner is greedy and obsessive. Worst of all, he's prideful. Unable to admit failure. These are all qualities that are exceedingly rare among the Alvearu. They are indeed more common in shapeshifters, and among humans, they run rampant."

"We're not who you think we are."

"Yes, you are," he said. "Not all of you, mind you, but enough. We prey on these weaknesses. This is how the doctor convinced the people of Earth to turn over their fellow humans for his experiments. This is how the doctor made a deal with your grandfather so many years ago. He gave the doctor permission to mind control the Martian majority in exchange for terraforming expertise, wasn't that the deal?"

"It was," I said, feeling the usual dark stir in my gut whenever that particular subject was broached. I'd learned to forgive the man, but knowing deep down that I would never have betrayed my people like that still made my cheeks burn in shame.

"Now I've grown quite fond of all of you sitting at this table, and I know you represent some of the best of your kind, but I also know that as strong and surprising as humans can be, you're also guilty of destroying your own planet."

"Don't act like your kind is perfect. The hive must have a weakness. What is it?"

"First off, it's not a single hive. It's billions of unique hives that coordinate and cross-pollinate. Second, if you're looking for a weakness, there isn't one. This is why the spread of the Alvearu across the galaxy continues thousands of years after it started. The Alvearu welcome those who are capable of hiving and those who aren't become drones through mind control."

"Except for us."

"Except for you. Other than the sledgehammer of a mind control system implemented by the doctor on Earth, your brains seem impervious." He put a hand over his heart. "I'm sorry to say, Earth and Mars will be taken, and you'll be wiped out anyway."

"Oh, you're sorry now?" snapped Navya.

"Personally, yes, I truly am. But your fate is inevitable. The entire galaxy will one day be an Alvearu singularity."

"This is what the Alvearu want?" I asked. "To turn the entire galaxy into a giant hive?"

"A third of the galaxy already is."

"Wait," said Nigel, "I want to go back to what you said about welcoming those who can hive. Does that mean that insects are never mind-controlled or exterminated?"

"Not all insects can hive, and not all who can hive are insects. But those who can are welcomed as equals. They have as much say as anybody else. Those who can't hive are considered inferior."

"Like humans."

"Yes, like humans."

"But what about botsies?" asked Nigel.

"What about them?"

Nigel laced his fingers together. "We can hive."

CHAPTER TWENTY-ONE

GHOST BLINKED. THEN BLINKED AGAIN. "WHAT do you mean botsies can hive?"

"I built a communication system," said Nigel. "It allows us to not only communicate with each other, but to feel each other's emotions. It's only been installed in a hundred of us so far, but it makes us a hive."

Now, I was the one who was blinking. When it came to making peace with the aliens, I felt a ray of hope for the very first time. Nigel had created a hive of botsies. A *hive*.

"Can you prove this?" asked Ghost.

"Of course, I can."

"Show me."

"Come to my cabin and I'll call up the schematics."

"Wait," I said. "I wasn't done with Ghost. We need to decide what to do with him. We know we can't trust him."

"I've already decided," said Nigel. "He's part of our

crew, and he's going to help us make a case to the Alvearu that botsies and humans should be spared."

"Since when do you make the decisions?"

"Since you made me captain. Let me show you those schematics, Ghost."

They both stood and exited the galley, leaving Navya and me to stare at each other. "What just happened?" I asked.

"Welcome to my world," she said with a sly grin.

"There it is," said Ghost. "The gate."

"Where?"

"Those three rocks right there." The trio Ghost pointed to looked like any other rocks in the asteroid belt. "They might look like rocks, but the gate dwellers are quite similar to your scarab beetles, only on a massive scale. They're covered in something akin to barnacles which gives them their craggy texture."

"Can you talk to them?" asked Navya.

"I've been talking to them for hours," said Ghost. "They're quite chatty. Denver, you should practice before we pass through to the other side."

I nodded and tried to see through one of the massive creature's eyes. Ghost had spent a few hours each day for the last several weeks tutoring me on how to make the connection. I'd gotten pretty good at connecting to Ghost's eyes and even succeeded in seeing through the doctor's eyes the handful of times I'd tried. With the doctor, I never stayed in for more than a second or two. Remain longer and Ghost had warned he might detect my presence, and realize he could return the favor by tapping into my eyes whenever he liked. As long as he didn't suspect my eyes had been replaced with alien eyes, he'd have no reason to try the tap at all.

I took another long look at the gate dwellers on screen, and like Ghost had taught me, I crossed my eyes slightly, just enough to bring them out of focus and concentrated on a mental image of the being I wanted to tap into. "It's not working," I said.

"Try again."

I stood up from my seat and jumped up and down for a thirty second count. As it turned out, I didn't need to be scared or terrified to make the connection, but some additional oxygen and an elevated heartbeat certainly made it easier.

After sitting back down and taking a few deep breaths, I tried the eye-tap again, and was rewarded with a view of space. Feeling unanchored, I gripped my armrests. "I'm in."

"What do you see?" asked Ghost.

"Stars and rocks," I said. Now that I was seeing from one of the gate dweller's eyes, the hard part was finding a focal point in my thousand-fold view. I couldn't.

"Good. You never know when that skill might give you an edge."

I needed all the edge I could get. In less than five minutes, we'd be through the gate and would come face to face with the alien outpost. From there, the plan was to split into two groups. Nigel and Ghost would head to the leadership council to state their case for recognizing botsies as hive-capable. Amazingly, Ghost had made an appointment. Who knew you could call ahead and arrange such a thing? Nigel was right to welcome Ghost to our crew.

The other group would consist of Smith, the doctor, Ojiisan and me. The doctor had secretly arranged to borrow a lab from a sister—he had dozens of siblings—that had all the equipment he'd need to transfer Smith's AI into Ojiisan's mind. Navya would stay with the ship.

I heard Nigel hobble in, the step-drag-step of his walking pattern instantly recognizable. Quickly, I detached from the gate dwellers. "Ready?" I asked him.

"As I'll ever be," he said. "I rehearsed my presentation all night." He put a hand on Ghost's shoulder. "You really think we have a chance?"

"I do," said Ghost. "I'm proud to be your sponsor."

I believed him when he said that. Despite it all, I had to admit I really did trust Ghost. Not that I didn't need some convincing. It was Nigel who had pushed me in the right direction late that same night he decided to recognize Ghost as a member of our crew. I remembered his words exactly. "It starts with us," he said, my hands gripped in his. "If we can't make peace with Ghost then what hope do humanity and the Alvearu have?"

I was right to make Nigel our captain.

"Two minutes to the gate," said Ghost. He looked excited. Sponsoring a new hive was an honor among the Alvearu. More than an honor. From what he'd shared about his kind, this was the sort of thing that would earn him a parade no matter where he went, maybe even get a planet named in his honor. This was the kind of thing that would land his carapace in the Alvearu's most hallowed museum when he passed on. Sponsoring the botsie hive would provide more reward than he could ever spend in a long lifetime.

If not for the promise of great fanfare, he might not have contentedly agreed to miss out on collecting a bounty for bringing the doctor in to face trial. Still, he'd proven time and again to be a productive member of our team. Beyond teaching me how to do the eye-tap, he'd given us a series of daily one-hour presentations about the Alvearu. We'd all learned so much from those briefings about our adversary's biology, history, and culture. He would always stay until he'd answered every last question we could ask. Dare I say, I'd begun to think of him as a close friend?

Despite a wealth of doubts, he remained optimistic that botsies would gain hive status. Where that left humanity was anybody's guess, but it was Nigel's hope that crediting humans as botsie creators would at the very least convince the Alvearu to cancel extermination orders.

Of course, all of this was still a longshot. Nigel was an artificial lifeform. A computer. A robot. I'd come to realize he and the other botsies were so much more than that, but I was ashamed to say it took me many years to arrive at that conclusion. We needed the Alvearu to come to the same realization right now. Mars City was still under attack. The news reports sounded more and more dire every day, the latest turn of bad news coming in the form of an attack on Mars's food supply. Almost half of the agri-platforms had been devastated by locusts. That was what people were calling them, anyway. In truth, these bugs were much smaller than their biblical namesakes. Seemingly harmless at the size of a mite, they were completely devastating when counted in the millions.

The little stowaways clung to clothes and reproduced at such a staggering rate that entire agri-platforms were laid to waste before anybody knew what was happening. Strict decontamination procedures seemed to have stopped them from spreading any farther, but a fifty percent reduction in food was going to starve thousands.

"Thirty seconds," said Ghost.

I watched out the window. We were finally close enough to the gate dwellers to see some definition to their shapes. Instead of pocked boulders, they now resembled scarabs just as Ghost had promised. Ghost steered us toward the center of their triangular formation and their abdomens started to glow and pulse. Bolts of electricity arced between them, and then we were through to the other side.

"Just like that," said Ghost with a snap of his fingers.

"Jesus," said Navya, pointing to a giant blip on the display. "It's huge."

Ghost turned the ship, and the outpost filled our view through the windshield. "It has spots," I said as if that was somehow more remarkable than its immensity. The spots were an inky black while the rest of it was a mesmerizingly iridescent array of blues, yellows and greens that seemed to shift and ripple in the light of a bright sun. Never before had I been so thankful to be able to see color. The outpost's shape was so full of twists, spirals and corkscrews that it defied any kind of categorization. "It's really alive?" I asked.

"It is," said Ghost. "Four hundred years old and should survive for at least another two centuries. In another fifty years or so, it will be time for it to mate so a new one can grow and eventually take its place."

"Where's its head?" asked Navya.

"It doesn't have one," said Ghost. "Its mind is near the center, and it was engineered to grow itself outward from there."

"Does it eat?"

"It soaks up energy from the sun. All outposts like these are near a bright star. The minerals it needs to grow are pulverized before being fed into a root system."

"So, it's a plant?"

He shrugged like he always did when he didn't have an answer. We were going to have to create a whole new dictionary in order to describe the Alvearu.

Ghost spoke into the radio, his words a mix of clicks

and slithery hisses. "Requesting permission to dock," he said to the rest of us in English.

"Those rocks over there, is that another gate?" asked Nigel.

Ghost nodded. "There are four gates here. Some locations have dozens with thousands of ships passing through every day. This outpost is very remote in comparison. The worlds you can get to from here are all still in the early stages of terraforming and development.

An unintelligible message came through the speaker. "We're all set," said Ghost as he grabbed the ship's controls. "Alvearu ships are guided in by autopilot, but this ship can't interface with its guidance systems."

Flashes of bright blue electricity webbed up and down the outpost's entire length. Bright bolts made me blink, and even then, they left a ghostly impression on my retinas for several seconds after it stopped. "Whoa," I said. "What was that?"

"Lightning. One of the most populous species comes from a world that's ravaged by electrical storms. They become unsettled when their light source remains consistent for too long. Those who live aboard have windows installed so they can be calmed by the storms when they come every ten minutes or so."

"The doctor must be of that same species."

"No, he's a shapeshifter like me, but he spent his formative years on such a world and must've gained an affinity for it. Many of us have."

I turned to Navya, whose face was lit with the wonder

of this mind-boggling place, and I supposed I was just as awed, but I cautioned myself against being seduced any farther. For now, they were still our enemy.

Ghost angled us into the outpost's shadow. Away from the glinting sun, I tried to make out the outpost's winding contours but it was difficult to find a place to anchor my eye. Instead, my view got lost in seashells, screws, and spirals like those of fiddlehead ferns. Waves of honeycomb came into view to tickle hairy growths that rippled like fields of wheat despite the lack of wind. Taken all together, the outpost was dizzyingly immense, and impossibly difficult to digest. Like cramming an entire ocean of life into a single tableau and asking, what do you see?

The ship glided toward a stop, the docking ring at our vessel's nose now entering a group of spidery legs that began to twitch and move. "Ovipositors," said Ghost.

"Ovi-whats?"

"Ovipositors. They're used to lay eggs, though these eggs are unfertilized. I have to run off to my cabin to change," said Ghost. "Meet you at the airlock in a couple minutes."

He stepped out leaving the rest of us to watch globby, gooey eggs spouting forth to stick to the steel docking ring.

"They must use it to create a seal," said Nigel.

Quickly, they began to fill up the space between our ship and the iridescent wall of the outpost.

"Gross," said Navya.

I laughed. "I was about to say the same thing."

Nigel stood. "That right there might be our biggest challenge."

"What's that?"

"If we manage to broker a peace with them, we're going to have to work to control ourselves when it comes to the ick factor. We have to accept them as people, not as something that makes us squeal and grab the nearest flyswatter."

I looked at the thick, gelatinous sealant piling up outside and couldn't suppress a shiver. "Easier said than done."

One at a time, we went down the ladder connecting the ship's bridge to the airlock to wait for Ghost to change clothes. "You can do this," I told Nigel. "Wish I could go with you."

"I'll do my best," he said.

"Never had any doubt of that."

Navya grabbed him in a fierce hug. On the journey here, I thought she was making good progress getting over him, but her sparkling eyes said something different. "Good luck," she said.

She waved me in, and I joined the three-way embrace. I had no idea what the next few hours held in store for Ojiisan, Smith, and the rest of humanity, but with friends like these, I'd be able to weather whatever came my way. I let myself sink into the warmth of the embrace, but then I felt a hand tense on my back. I pulled back far enough to see that Navya's face had frozen in shock. Or was it fear? I reached for my holster.

<It's okay, Denver,> said Smith. <It's Ghost.>

Slowly, I turned around. It was Ghost. But I'd never seen him like this. He had six legs. Only the first four were on the deck so he was halfway standing upright. His hands were pincers, and a segmented scorpion tail curled up to hang over his head.

"It's me." Ghost's voice was choppy and lacking breath, his mouthparts not quite capable of sounding human. "Why are you all so shocked? I told you I was going to my cabin to change."

CHAPTER TWENTY-TWO

"A SCORPION?" I ASKED. "REALLY?"

"You don't like it? I wanted to do something to represent your home planet."

"Why don't you just go as yourself?" I answered my own question before he could respond. "Wait, I remember what you said. Shapeshifters have been around so long they don't remember what they originally looked like."

His head tipped downward. I took it as an affirmative.

"Ready?" Nigel asked.

"What? No hugs for me?" asked Ghost. He made a clicking sound that I hoped was a laugh before opening the airlock's inner hatch. "I've adjusted our air pressure to match theirs so no need to cycle." He opened the outer hatch to expose the hull of the alien outpost. Using his pincers, he cut into the wall.

"What the hell are you doing?"

"How else would we get in? The hole will heal up as

soon as we depart." Having created a tear, he and Nigel peeled the shell away in chunks. I picked up a piece of it and was surprised to see how thin and light it felt in my hands.

The opening was plenty big enough to walk through, and I could see the welcome party standing on the ceiling. Ghost had assured us the outpost used artificial gravity, but like most bugs, the spindly, spidery beings weren't limited to walking on the floor like gravity preferred.

I recognized them from one of Ghost's lectures. The Oroly. Bureaucrats. I smiled and gave them a nervous wave as if either gesture would be recognized as friendly. Nigel and Ghost stepped across the egg barrier that blinked like a blue neon sign from one of the electrical storms outside.

Unintelligible words were exchanged, and Ghost turned back to say, "They want you to undock. They don't want anybody else sneaking on board."

Navya nodded her understanding, and we watched them go through what looked to be a garden of geometric patterned sculptures before disappearing around a corner.

Navya closed the hatch. "I'll start the undocking procedure."

"I'll get the doctor," I said.

Navya held the syringe. "Ready?" She asked the doctor. He nodded.

With no effort to be gentle, she jabbed the needle into his neck and depressed the plunger. Nanobots.

We'd recovered some from Ojiisan's body and reprogrammed them to accept orders from the same transmission system I used to talk to Smith. We told the doctor they would manufacture cyanide if I gave the command.

The part about the poison was a ruse. If such a thing was possible, none of us—not even Nigel—had the skills to pull it off, but the hope was it was plausible enough to keep the doctor under control when I inevitably had to relinquish my weapon to him so he could transfer Smith into Ojiisan. Just in case, though, I stowed a pulseripper in an ankle holster for extra insurance.

Navya pulled the needle free and gave me a quick hug before exiting the cargo bay.

"To get us inside, I'm going to need a tool to cut through the outpost's exoskeleton," Werner said.

"What kind of tool?"

"Something sharp." He eyed a vibra-blade sitting on a nearby bench.

"Fat chance," I said.

"If you want this plan of yours to work, you're going to have to trust me with much sharper objects when I start operating on your grandfather. Plus," he pointed at the injection mark on his neck, "cyanide, right?"

<What do you think, Smith?>

<He's right, Denver. We're going to have to trust him. We don't have much of a choice.>

I sighed and grabbed the vibra-blade from the bench.

"No funny business," I said before handing him the blade. "Or I'll see to it that those nanobots make it slow and agonizing for you." I locked my helmet in place and waited for Doctor Werner to do the same before opening the airlock to the void of space. I checked the tethers one more time then rolled my grandfather's body out into zero-g.

I spoke into the radio. "Receiving Smith's feed?"

"Absolutely," replied Navya. "Nigel's feed is strong too. I'll be monitoring you both every step of the way."

Smith spoke into my mind. <Even after the doctor transfers me into Ojiisan, the equipment in the gun should keep transmitting.>

I turned to the doctor and patted my holster. "Remember, I'll tell him to unleash those nanobots if I have to."

He nodded inside his faceshield.

"Let's roll," I said.

We both jumped out, and I reeled in my grandfather's tethers and cinched them tight so he wouldn't whiplash around when I engaged the jetpack.

I saw the massive creature functioning as an alien outpost floating in the distance. The lab was housed somewhere inside of it. I started to question which was crazier: the mission or myself for agreeing to it. Werner jetted toward the outpost, and I struggled to follow, the extra weight of my grandfather making it difficult to navigate.

<Let me,> said Smith.

I gladly turned control over to him, and my flight path began to stabilize. <I'm going to miss you helping me out like this.>

<I know. I'm scared I won't know what to do with myself without you getting us into trouble all the time.>

These last few weeks in transit, Smith had become more responsive. We'd had several long discussions about his upcoming transition, each and every one of them making me feel better about my decision to allow the transfer into Ojiisan. It still bothered me that he'd seized control of the ship, but I'd learned through our discussions just how desperate he was. Tough as it was to imagine an AI being depressed and paranoid, it was an apt description. Nigel was correct when he had said Smith was fighting for survival.

Since I'd given Smith permission to inhabit my grandfather's vessel—that was how Smith had begun referring to Ojiisan's body—he'd been a model citizen. In the end, I was the one who apologized for ignoring and minimizing his dire distress thereby forcing him to go so far as hijacking the ship. I couldn't say for sure if this next chapter in his life would repair his identity, but I'd been thoroughly convinced that anything was better than where he was, which was a shattered existence overrun with doubt and fear.

Smith slowed our pace as I trailed the doctor to a large, translucent windowpane that reminded me of a dragonfly's wing. Inside, I could see a figure with numerous big, oily eyes, multiple clacking mandibles, and antennae stretching out like spider legs. Doctor Werner's sister.

The doctor pulled the blade from his pocket and made to cut his way through the partitioned window. But his sister seemed to be shooing us away by making sweeping motions with her antennae.

By the time I reached for the jetpack's controls, Smith's speedier reflexes already had me moving backward. The doctor's jets engaged just as I saw sparks emerging from the nose of the alien outpost. Bursting forth from its cavernous nostrils like fire after a freshly tossed log, the sparks zipped down the length of the alien outpost. Within seconds, the entire surface of the station was alive with blinding lightning. A painful crackling of static sounded from my helmet speakers, and I felt the hair on my arms stand up. I kept moving backward, terrified that a bolt from the electrical storm was going to arc across the gap to fry me inside my suit. It lasted for at least a minute. The flashes of white-hot energy looked like bare trees blinking in and out of existence. Finally, the crackle of my speakers began to subside, and the glowing forest of electricity encasing the outpost petered out.

The doctor and I jetted back toward the window to try to sneak inside before the next round fired up. Reaching the organic windowpane, the doctor used his blade to cut an X. Using his jets, he pushed his way through, then finding a handhold to grasp onto, he helped to pull me and Ojiisan inside, where the artificial gravity yanked us to the floor. Werner passed through a sheet of green light, then took off his helmet. "You'll be able to breath on this side of the forcefield."

I dragged Ojiisan through the rippling green sheet that kept the outpost's atmosphere from blowing out. I popped the seal on my helmet and took a deep breath of air that smelled faintly of honey. Looking back, I saw the outer membrane was already healing itself.

Werner's sister used a flurry of caterpillar-like legs to help the doctor out of his suit, leaving me to struggle with my grandfather and his tethers. I finished the job just in time to see the doctor begin his transition. His head elongated, and multiple eyes expanded to become black pools of tar. Mandibles clicked and clacked where his jaw had been. Arms and legs narrowed and segmented, tarsal claws sprouting where ankles and wrists once stood. His torso elongated and cinched like a tourniquet at the waist to separate thorax from abdomen.

We were in a small lab with holographic screens lighting up an entire wall. Recessed shelves were topped by tidy stacks of labeled bins. Another wall was lined with neatly arranged equipment—microscopes, centrifuges, and fume hoods.

"She's a lot more organized than you are," I told the doctor.

He didn't bother to acknowledge me, but instead held out a hand. I took Smith from my holster and placed him upon the doctor's sticky pad.

"Help me put your grandfather on the table," he ordered.

After getting Ojiisan into position, I turned to find myself face-to-face with Werner's sister. Her mouthparts moved like blades of a paper shredder as her antennae made the same shooing motion as I'd seen before. I backed up to the wall where I could stay out of the way.

Now that the exterior window had finished patching itself up, she turned off the shimmering green forcefield before attaching electrodes to Ojiisan's head. I couldn't help but find it strange that she and her brother didn't talk to each other. After so many years apart, why such a cold greeting?

I almost said something about it, but thankfully realized how dumb I'd sound before I did. They were hive animals capable of communicating on a wavelength we humans couldn't detect. For all I knew, they'd been having a jolly old time since we first came inside.

<Still there, Smith?>

<Yes. They're still patching into me. Then it will take some time for them to create the proper interface to give me control of the vessel. I'll go dark when they begin the transfer.>

<Can you patch me into Nigel's feed?>

CHAPTER TWENTY-THREE

I COULD SEE WHAT NIGEL SAW. HE WAS IN A cavernous room with bright spotlights shining down on him. Hundreds of black, beady eyes embedded in the walls functioned as cameras for the various hives watching throughout the galaxy. To his right stood Ghost and straight ahead was a single Alvearu standing at a jade altar that hovered before a tower of honeycomb.

"Now that your presentation is complete," said the judge with a low-pitched growl that sounded more like a hungry stomach than a voice. "Questioning may commence."

All was silent for a few, long minutes. As Ghost had told us, the Alvearu would collect questions from the hives, and then a short period of debate would begin.

The judge momentarily phosphoresced, a signal that the first question was in. "If you are indeed capable of hiving, why did you come before us as a single representative?"

"For the same reason your honor acts as the single magistrate for the tribunal process," said Nigel. "It only takes one of us to communicate."

More silence ensued as a follow-up question was formulated. "Your diagrams and flowcharts appear to be in order, but proof of hive capability can only come from hiving with others of your kind, and then with the Alvearu. Yet you are the only botsie standing before us. How can we judge your fitness for hive status if we're unable to confirm you can indeed hive?"

"I can go get others and come before you again in two months' time. With your help, we can adapt our hive system to interface with yours and prove without a shadow of a doubt that botsies can hive just like you. In the meantime, I request you stop your attacks on Mars."

Another long pause before the next question. "You admit you are an artificial lifeform. However, the Alvearu have never allowed non-biological beings, such as botsies, to be equals. Why should we reconsider?"

This time it was Ghost who responded. "Many in the Alvearu were manufactured through genetic or bioengineering programs just like this space station. Whether it was by evolution or by design, all that matters is the botsies have that rarest of sparks. Not only are they intelligent, but they can hive. How they arrived is immaterial."

<Disconnect me,> I told Smith. Much as I wanted to follow the proceedings, I needed to keep an eye on what was happening here lest I forget Doctor Werner was the

king of double-dealing treachery. At some point, he'd make a move, and I needed to stay alert enough to catch it.

My grandfather had been turned facedown, and Werner was working fibers into the back of his neck to go under the skull and up into his brain. His sister worked at the keyboards, four of them at the same time.

A moth, or something like it, fluttered past me. "You have moths here?" I asked.

"Yes," said the doctor. His real voice was low and slow and soaked with a droning quality that reminded me of a cicada. "We have pests, too, unfortunately."

"Well, if this doesn't work," I said, tapping my ankle holster. "You'll be getting a personal lesson in pest control."

"I'm not just doing this to save myself, Denver. I'm as curious as you are to see if it actually works."

"That sounds about right. Just another way of manipulating the human mind to you, isn't it?"

He made a gurgling noise that I took for a laugh.

Flashes of light made me shade my eyes as another lightning storm raged outside.

<They'll begin the transfer soon,> said Smith. <Shutdown is imminent.>

<Are you afraid?>

<More excited than afraid. Even if this goes poorly, at least I will have taken the leap. Thank you for allowing this, and I apologize again for seizing the ship's controls. Please don't hold it against him.>

<Him?>

<The new Smith.>

<I won't,> I told him.

<I think his name will be—> He didn't get the chance to finish.

I had to laugh at the timing of it. What a way to keep me in suspense.

That was it. The last time we'd ever speak directly into each other's minds. Gradually, my smile melted and my heart grew heavy with the fact that Ojiisan and Smith, the two people in my life who were closest to me, were both gone. I buoyed myself knowing they'd soon be combined into something new. Whatever his name turned out to be, he was a person I couldn't wait to meet.

Doctor Werner was standing behind his sister now, his head moving as he read from the displays. He pointed at something, and his sister worked at the keyboard to adjust for whatever anomaly he'd spotted. A progress bar lit up on one of the screens, and I knew the transfer had begun.

"Is that it?" I asked.

"That's it," said the doctor. "Now we wait to see if he wakes up after completion."

I nervously tapped my fingers. I really wished Smith had agreed to make a backup of himself before the transfer, but he insisted this be a one-way street. He'd either emerge from this as a coherent and sane AI-person or the experiment would fail, and I'd disable the nanobots keeping my grandfather's body alive and let Smith pass from this world.

Another moth fluttered past and disappeared into the wall. That couldn't be, could it? I moved closer to see that it hadn't actually melted into the wall, but its maple syrup color was such a close match to the beetle-shell room divider it was near perfectly camouflaged. When I got too close, the moth flew away.

I followed it to one of the refrigeration units. Upon reaching the metallic surface, the moth took on a silver sheen. Amazing. If Nigel and Ghost were successful, I looked forward to many more wonders about the Alvearu yet to be discovered.

I turned back to see that the doctor and his sister had traded places. The doctor now sat at the keyboard, and the doctor's sister was watching me. I was about to ask if she wanted something, when she abruptly pivoted and left the room, leaving the doctor and me to wait for the progress bar to complete.

He took a couple steps toward the exit, and I instinctively moved a hand toward my ankle holster. "Where are you going?" I knew as well as he did that the communication system in my head had a limited range. If he could get far enough away from me, I'd lose my ability to control the nanobots. Of course, they weren't capable of unleashing deadly cyanide like he thought, but I needed to keep up appearances.

He stopped and opened a refrigerator. He pulled out a jar of a thick, mucky liquid. "What's that for?" I asked.

He dropped a proboscis into the jar. "Thirsty," he said

over audible slurping.

My fingers twitched and began to relax. My eyes darted to the progress bar. Almost done.

"Any second now," he said, "and my side of the deal will be honored."

"Then you'll be free to go."

A few more tense moments passed before the progress bar reached the end. The transfer was complete. Ojiisan—no, Smith, opened his eyes for a second or two before closing them again. My heart fluttered. For a moment, I was convinced that my grandfather was finally coming to. That my mission to save him was a success. But a second later, logic set in, and I knew that was nothing more than wishful thinking. Still, seeing signs of life coming from his unresponsive body made me hopeful. It was all such a mindfuck.

"Smith?" I asked. "Can you hear me?"

He nodded, but the motion was stilted and jerky, like he was struggling to learn how to do it. "I hear you," he said in my grandfather's voice, his speech froggy but otherwise understandable.

Werner put his drink back in the fridge and walked to the exit. "My work is done," he said. "Goodbye."

"Goodbye and good riddance, Doctor Werner."

His mouthparts ground and his antennae straightened. "I'll pass your goodbye along."

The gears in my own head began to grind. "What does that mean?"

"He already left." And then he...no, not he. She disappeared through the exit, and it constricted and closed behind her.

How the hell did they pull that off? When I was studying that damned moth was when. I thought they'd traded places, but they stayed right where they were—her at the keyboard and him standing behind—and traded shapes instead. Then the doctor slipped away and out of range of the transmission system in my head. Clever bastard.

"The nanobots can't make cyanide anyway!" I shouted to no one. Since we'd made our deal, I'd been assuming that he couldn't evade the Alvearu authorities for long, but the shapeshifter just might be devious enough to stay on the lam indefinitely.

"Can you get these straps off?" asked Smith, but I was slow to respond as a creeping anxiety stretched for my throat. The doctor had executed a shrewd escape, but what else might he have planned? Crossing my eyes, I reached out to Werner and tapped into his eyes.

My view splintered into a thousand cells as I saw from his compound vision. Inside each of those cells, I saw bugs. Dozens of them—the same unintelligent soldier bugs that were attacking Mars City—lined up in front of him. A hundred more were bursting from egg sacs suspended from the ceiling.

I hurried to undo Smith's chest straps. "We gotta get out of here. Now!"

With hands freed, Smith grunted as he yanked the filaments from his head. Seeing my grandfather move again made me stop in my tracks. I felt the sudden urge to hug him, but immediately shook off the notion. This wasn't Ojiisan, and I had to accept that.

I made a beeline for where our spacesuits hung. Grabbing my suit, I found myself in a cloud of flitting, fluttering moths.

Oh shit.

I lifted a sleeve, and it was riddled with moth-eaten holes. I snatched another suit to find its thick layers eaten all the way through too.

The door the doctor's sister had exited just a couple minutes ago opened and a rush of bugs scrambled over each other to get inside.

CHAPTER TWENTY-FOUR

I PULLED MY WEAPON FROM MY ANKLE HOLSTER as the full dimensions of the doctor's betrayal came into focus. We were trapped in a room with only two ways out. One was through the door that was blocked off by a flood of incoming bugs. The other was through the window I'd entered an hour ago, which—thanks to sabotaged spacesuits—would lead out to the deadly vacuum of space.

Smith joined me, our backs pressed against the window. He wielded the Smith & Wesson he once called home and we both pumped our triggers as fast as we could. There was no way I was going to let him succumb to the same fate as Ojiisan. Bugs blew apart but others kept piling forward.

Vice-like mandibles dug into my knee and scissored through tendons and cartilage. I crushed the bug's shell with the butt of my pulseripper but the soft goo inside burned like acid and the 'ripper fell from my fingers.

I swung a fist, refusing to die any way other than fighting. Another bug bit into my shoulder and its spiny underside punctured my neck and cheek. Pincers reached for my throat, and I helplessly squirmed to avoid the deathblow.

The pincers viced shut short of my neck. Something had released behind me, and I was falling backward. A rush of wind hit me like the slap of a wave, and I was shot out into space.

Breath greedily sucked from my lungs and the moisture in my eyes instantly evaporated. I gulped for air that wasn't there as I continued to swing at the bugs that had latched onto me.

I glimpsed a suited figure holding a vibra-blade and saw a smile behind the faceshield.

Navya.

She had cut through the window to cause the decompression. A rush of bugs spewed out from the rupture, followed by any equipment in that lab that wasn't bolted down. A piece of gear struck Navya in the head. If I'd had any breath, it would've caught in my throat.

She reached for her helmet and locked it back in place. That was when I saw the burst of sparks. I screamed, but my voice was drowned by the void.

Smith and I flew into the cargo bay of Ghost's ship, and I barely got my legs in front of me to absorb some of the shock before slamming into the wall. I turned back to see if Navya had engaged her jets, but then a bolt struck, and then another. A bright confluence of energy collapsed into her and then she was gone—vaporized in an instant.

I screamed again. Beads of blood spilled like pearls from several wounds as bugs kept gnawing on my flesh. One blew apart, and I was vaguely aware of a suited Nigel engaged in battle.

The doors of the cargo bay began to close.

As did my eyelids.

CHAPTER TWENTY-FIVE

I WOKE IN A MED LAB. MY RIGHT HAND WAS cocooned in see-through regen patches. Two fingers were missing, sliced off clean by one of the bug's razor-sharp mandibles. My left leg was splinted, my knee encased in more regen patches. I had bandages on my shoulder. One around my ankle and another on my foot. When I felt under my robe, I found several more along my ribcage.

I looked to my right. Smith was there, sitting in a chair, a bandage on his forehead. He had the same concerned look in his eyes that I was so used to seeing on Ojiisan. He stood and came to me.

"Navya?" I asked.

He looked down and with the slimmest shake of his head, he confirmed my worst fear. I hadn't been hallucinating before passing out. She was gone. Incinerated by the lightning storm.

"I'm sorry," he said.

I closed my eyes, tears leaking out. "Where are we?"

"We've gone back through the gate. Course set for Mars. Do you feel strong enough to go to the bridge? You've been under for almost twenty-four hours, and there's much to catch you up on."

I wiped tears from my cheeks. "Give me a minute." Navya was dead. Lost in an effort to save me. The pain in my heart was so much heavier than the pain emanating from my many wounds. She was my friend. My sister. My hero.

Smith handed me a tissue. "Take all the time you need."

"How's your head?" I asked him.

"Fine," he said. "I'm saner than I've ever been. I finally feel," he paused to find the right word, "integrated."

"You're sure?"

"Before the transfer, I was adrift on stormy seas. My world is smaller now. I'm in a calm little inlet where my thoughts come one at a time instead of billions every second."

I took his hand. "Let's be thankful for that."

I thought he'd looked like Ojiisan earlier, and he did when it came to physical features, but it was also obvious now that he was not Ojiisan. I could see it in the uncanny way he cocked his head and how he hugged his shoulders to his neck. His lips were tightened into a thin line, and his eyes were squinched in the corners. I couldn't remember a similar facial expression ever appearing on my grandfather.

"Of the two of us, I guess you got the worst of it," he said. Even his voice was off now, closer to a monotone instead of my grandfather's calm but expressive lilt.

I pointed at the bandage on his head. "Is that all you got?"

"I have a nasty gash under my pantleg, and there's a deep divot in my shoulder."

"You've never felt pain before."

"It's most unpleasant," he said. "But there's a novelty to it that I'm quite enjoying. Come. Let's get you to the bridge."

I struggled to sit up and let him help me into a hover-chair, my leg sticking straight out front.

"The knee joint is bad," he said. "You won't be able to walk until you get proper surgery back home."

"Before the transfer, you didn't get the chance to tell me your new name."

He pushed me toward the door. "Masato Moon."

"Ojiisan's father. My great-grandfather."

"Yes. It felt right to honor the family as long as you don't object."

"I like it," I said. "Masato."

Exiting into the corridor, he guided me to the lift that hauled us to the bridge. Ghost was at the controls. Nigel sat right next to him, still wearing the spacesuit that was badly damaged in the fight. He hobbled over to me as soon as we entered. Somehow, despite the obstacles of each of our bum legs, he managed to bend low and hug me in my chair.

"I'm so sorry about Navya," he said.

"You loved her too."

He pulled back to look me in the eyes. "That I did. She was my first and only true romance. I've never met a better person."

The tears were flowing again. Even Nigel's eyes had misted up, which I never knew was possible.

"I hate to cut this short," said Ghost. "But we have urgent matters to discuss." He pushed a button, and a holographic display lit the space between us. I saw ships. A fleet of them. "War hornets," he said. "They came through the gate an hour ago. We have almost a day's head start but they're faster than this bucket. They'll overtake us in three days."

"And if they do?"

"The hornets are laden with nukes. As soon as they get close enough to fire, they will. We'll be destroyed."

"Wait," I said, finding it difficult to unpack this new development. "What the hell happened when you tried to get botsies approved as hive beings?"

"Our application was a failure," he said. "They couldn't understand why Nigel would come before them without absolute proof that he can hive. We should've gone to Mars after Earth to pick up more botsies so they could be observed hiving with each other."

"Mars is under attack. Going back to there to get more botsies would've delayed us by two months. Mars City could be wiped out by then."

"We made it a point to describe our extenuating

circumstances, but the hives are sometimes known to ignore evidence in a rush to judgment. I was tapped into the collective when it all happened. There was a small but noisy few on the fringe who posited that we might be perpetuating a fraud in order to save Mars. Once that notion caught on, it snowballed and spread through the hives like wildfire."

"Groupthink."

"Yes. That's the very nature of the Alvearu. Our application was rejected, and we were dismissed back to our ship. After Navya redocked to pick us up, we ignored the mandated flight path and moved into position to pick you up. Navya suited up and was about to go EVA when Doctor Werner's attack began. She was monitoring your situation closely the whole time."

"I'm sure she was," I said, my voice barely audible. I felt moisture rising in my eyes again, and a frog lifting in my throat, but I forced myself to swallow it back down. "Okay, so now we go back to Mars to bring back more botsies, right?"

"Yes, that was Nigel's determination, but then this." He gestured at the warships.

"Can we evade them? Find a little hiding spot on a nearby asteroid or something?"

Nigel said, "No. Their tracking technology is too good. We've already worked through a hundred different scenarios, and they all end the same way, with us getting a nuke up our tailpipe."

"Why are they after us?"

"We've been declared extremists," said Ghost.

I just about jumped out of my chair, bad leg and all. "What?"

"They're accusing us of sabotage. They think our application for hive status was meant as a diversion for the attack on the outpost."

"The doctor's bugs attacked us, not the other way around."

"I'm well aware, but they think differently."

"Was the decompression even that bad?"

"No. Forcefields were brought up rather quickly so only a very small section of the outpost was damaged. Other than the soldier ants, nobody was hurt either or they'd be calling us murderers. Still, they take a harsh view on vandalism of any type. We were damn lucky to get through the gate at all. We probably made it through just a minute or two before they would've shut it down."

"They've got the wrong end of the stick," said Nigel. "But no matter how unjust their decisions, they have banks of missiles ready to take us out."

Masato stepped into the hologram to study the arrays of missiles attached to sprawling wings. "So many missiles. We have to assume that when they finish with us, they'll move on to destroy Mars."

"Be done with us once and for all," I said.

CHAPTER TWENTY-SIX

MY BODY WAS SORE FROM LYING IN BED so long. The clock said it was late afternoon, yet I stayed where I was.

It had been two days of mourning. A gut-wrenching forty-eight hours of anguish. Meals were glum affairs of few words and diminished appetites. The bridge sat empty much of the time, the constant dwindle of the countdown timer a depressing reminder of how little time we had left before being obliterated by a nuclear weapon.

When it struck, at least it would be quick. Like Navya. I'd shed so many tears for her, though as time wore on, just as many were shed for Mars. My grandfather's life's work.

Who was I kidding? It was my life's work, too. All of it destroyed for eternity.

I held out hope that the warning messages we'd been transmitting would save at least a few who might be able to flee aboard a ship or dig a bunker deep enough into Mars's crust to survive the bombing. But even if a few survived for years or decades, I knew the human race would perish. Losing Earth, our home world, was a self-inflicted wound too deep to recover from. We'd given Mars a try but were too weak to fend off the Alvearu's sustained attacks on our minds, then our bodies, and now our entire planet.

Mars was about to be destroyed, and there was nothing anybody could do to stop it.

That didn't keep Ghost and Nigel from trying. For the last two days, they worked on a system that could tap Nigel directly into the hive trailing us inside the war hornets, thus proving once and for all that botsies can hive. The first problem was Ghost didn't have a technical background. The second was Nigel didn't know a thing about the Alvearu or how they communicated. Despite the odds, they claimed to be close to a breakthrough.

However, even if they succeeded, there had to be, of course, another catch. After announcing that we'd been deemed terrorists when we first came through the gate, our pursuers had cut off all forms of communication. Even the hive-capable Alvearu transmitter Ghost had on board was totally useless if they refused to engage.

I forced myself to sit up and wrangled myself into my hoverchair. Masato might be on the bridge, and if so, maybe I could coax him into playing another game of Weichi with me. Now that he no longer had a quick-as-lightning computerized mind, I was actually able to edge him out last night. A rematch would at the very least give me the relief of occupying my mind for the next hour or so.

I went to the bridge and was disappointed to find Masato wasn't there. These last two days, his quirk of a smile was the lone bright spot in a haze of pain. How he stayed so positive was a mystery. I would've thought that finding himself trapped aboard this doomed vessel for the entirety of his short existence would send him straight back to despondency, but he kept himself buoyantly busy exploring new sights and smells despite their limited supply. He'd bent my ear for almost five minutes yesterday after popping open a can of oil in the engine room. *Now I know what viscous feels like* was the big takeaway.

I stared at the countdown timer looming onscreen. The war hornets would be in firing range in less than seven hours. Less than another half hour after that, the missiles would catch up to our maxed-out engines and that would be that. Surprisingly, my impending death didn't really bother me too much. It was when I thought of Navya, and the soon to be annihilated red planet that I felt most at despair.

The sensor screen showed a cluster of eight blips. Each one of those war hornets carried a nuclear payload powerful enough to destroy Mars a dozen times over.

I brought up a large hologram of Mars so I could look at her one more time. Slowly, it spun before me, the color of dried blood. I zoomed in on the domes over Mars City.

"I tried," I said. "We might've had a little more time if I hadn't insisted on annoying the bugs so much. I'm sorry about that. You were never much more than a subterranean rat maze, but you were a good home to me, and know that I've always done my best to serve you."

I watched the holo a little while longer before extinguishing it from view and sinking deep into my chair.

A new blip appeared on the sensor screen. This one was in front of us. I tapped on it to open a communication channel. "Whoever you are, you need to turn around," I said. "The bugs are coming your way."

A message on the screen read *requesting holo support.* I granted the request and a holographic blue dot appeared to my right. It hovered for a moment before wisps of smoke lifted from its radiant glow. Soon, the dot elongated to take the form of a cig-stick. The rest of him scrolled up from the floor, shiny boots, a gaudy fur coat, and bristly eyebrows.

"Jard?"

"It's me, Denver, and I brought help."

CHAPTER TWENTY-SEVEN

NIGEL, GHOST, AND MASATO ALL RUSHED IN TO join me on the bridge.

"I got your message," said Jard's hologram. "I brought twelve botsies who all have Nigel's communication modifications."

"Wait," I said, "what message?"

"Nigel sent me a message after you left Earth. He told me about the Alvearu and that his botsie communication system held the key to saving us all."

"Right," said Nigel. "Since you helped me build it, I wanted you to know, and I told you we were heading to the alien outpost to prove it."

"Yes, but then I thought, who's going to believe you if you go by yourself? You need more than one botsie to prove a communication system."

It was so damned obvious I couldn't help but laugh. I even bopped myself in the forehead with the heel of my hand, the universal gesture for *why didn't I think of that*.

"You're a little late," said Ghost. "But if you change direction, they may not follow you. After they finish us off, they'll continue heading straight to Mars."

"But I brought more botsies. Won't they stop attacking if we can prove botsies are enlightened with the capability to hive?"

"Yes," said Nigel. "But first we have to find a way to connect our botsie hive to the Alvearu so we can crossover to their minds. Even if we succeed, we have no way to prove it to them because they cut off all communications."

Jard put the cig-stick in his mouth. "You haven't figured out how to connect botsies to bugs?"

"No. We've been working on it, but the communication systems are so different, it's taking a long time to translate signals one by one."

"You don't need to do that," said Jard. "Just get the frequencies right, and they'll be able to hear you hiving with each other."

"But they won't be able to understand us."

"So what? We just have to prove you can hive, right? If they've incorporated thousands of hiving species, don't bother trying to translate your communications into something they can understand. Let them do the translating. They must be good at it."

"But we still can't transmit to them if they refuse to open a communication channel."

Jard puffed out a cloud of aqua-marine smoke. "They'll hear you if you go directly from mind to mind. Do that and it won't matter what they do with their radio transmitters."

"We can't get close enough for direct communication. We'd have to be within a few miles, but their nukes have a range of thousands of miles. We can't get anywhere near them without being destroyed."

"What if we tried to amplify signals by—"

"No," I interrupted. My pulse double-timed with excitement as the solution blossomed in my mind. "Here's the plan."

"They've launched," said Masato. "Two nukes, one for each of our ships."

"Impact?"

"Twenty-two minutes and thirteen seconds."

I called down to Ghost and Nigel. "Missiles launched. We better get a move on."

"Be right there, love," said Nigel.

Masato got to work on my leg. Using a pair of scissors, he cut away at the regen patches surrounding my knee while I worked at the patches enveloping my left hand. A rush of pain flooded in as the patches peeled away, but I bit it down. The patches had to go or I wouldn't be able to get into my spacesuit.

Nigel and Ghost entered and started to suit up. "How did it go?" asked Masato.

"Jard really is a wizard," said Nigel. "It only took him

two hours to make several hundred adjustments to our communications systems."

"Will it work? Will the Alvearu hear you?"

"We hope so. Won't know for sure until we rendezvous with the other botsies. Then we'll see if Ghost can hear us. If he can, it's a good bet the Alvearu on those ships will too if we can get close enough."

Masato helped me into my suit then hurried into his own. Ghost brought my helmet over and sat down next to me.

"You don't have to stay with us," I told him. "You're one of them. If you got in one of the escape pods, they might just stop and pick you up."

"I'll take my chances with you," he said. "I've staked a lot on proving botsies can hive, and I need to see it through. Plus, I've grown fond of you." He kissed my forehead before putting my helmet in place and locking it into its collar. He put his own helmet on, and I took his gloved hand and limped into the airlock.

I reached for the button to close the door, but Masato stopped me. "Wait," he said. "Let me check the calculations one more time."

"You've been checking and rechecking for the last several hours."

"I know, but I want to make sure they're correct."

It seemed he had a hard time trusting computer calculations when he couldn't do them himself anymore. "We can't wait," I told him. "Now's the time." I pushed the button, and the airlock door sealed shut. We waited for the light to flash, and Nigel spun the wheel to open the outer door.

Ghost was the first to make the leap, and I followed in short order. Masato and Nigel pushed off to join us. Jard's ship was only a hundred yards away, a sleek passenger vessel suspended before a blanket of stars. An airlock opened and the botsies floated out. Nobody bothered to close the airlock door. What would be the point?

With small bursts from our jetpacks, the two groups approached each other. The ships eased out ahead, and as programmed, launched into a maximum burn to draw the nukes as far ahead of us as possible.

The botsies joined arms, all thirteen of them in a ring. Nigel remained easy to pick out due to the crooked leg that made his suit's fabric stretch tight.

Jard jetted up to me, and—our faceshields slapping into each other—took me in his arms. "Denver!" he shouted through the radio. "It's great to see you."

We might all die out here as soon as our air ran out, but damn if I wasn't grinning ear-to-ear. "I've never been happier to see you!" I shouted back at the botstringer. "It all comes down to this. The entire history of the human race is either going to end here and now, or our greatest creation will come through to save us."

"I really hope it's the latter," said Jard. "If they pull this off, they'll all be emancipated in short order, don't you think? Mars will be protected because it's *their* world. Not ours."

"Emancipation will kill your business."

"Indeed, it will. But they deserve freedom."

"What will you do?"

"Somebody's going to have to help them build more botsies, right?"

"This is going to work, isn't it?"

"Damn straight it is," said Ghost. "I can hear the thirteen now. They're buzzing in my mind."

"Can you understand them?"

"Not in any literal sense, but I can feel their...their joy. I don't know how else to put it."

"The missiles," said Masato. "I can see them. We need to move a little. Sending instructions now."

Jetpacks engaged and our whole group moved in a coordinated thrust. "Jesus," said Jard. "They're coming right at us."

"We'll be fine," said Masato. "Don't panic and override your suit. It'll edge you out of harm's way all on its own."

The nukes streaked straight at us, leaving long contrails in their wake. Jard was right, it looked like we were going to be speared by the damn things. Maybe I should've let Masato recheck his calculations after all. The missiles continued to bear down on us at incredible speed, and I barely had time to gasp before they were past. A moment later, I felt the heat of their exhaust and found myself in a soupy cloud that evaporated in seconds.

"Damn, that was scary," I said.

"I know, but we need to stay as close as we can to the chase group's flight path. The war hornets need to fly right past us if they're going to hear the thirteen."

"How soon?" I asked.

"My calculations predict two minutes and eighteen seconds until they pass."

A flash of white-hot light blinded me.

"The nukes just detonated," said Masato. "Our ships are officially obliterated. We're going to take a heavy dose of radiation, but the radiation pills should minimize the damage."

I blinked until my vision came back. "You should've warned us how bright it was going to be."

"Sorry, I'm seeing spots too. I thought our faceplate's sun shielding would do a better job."

"Come close," said Nigel. "Join us. We're all in this together."

I jetted closer to the thirteen, the rest of my group doing the same. The circle of botsies separated to make room for us three humans and one Alvearu. I decided right then that this would be a fine way to die, stranded out here in the vast blackness of space. Such a contrast to a lifetime inside the tunnels.

 Those of us who relied solely on respiration would pass first. The botsies would survive a few weeks longer until their batteries ran out. No matter what happened, I was proud of how far we'd all come. If the thirteen failed, and Mars was to be annihilated, at least I could die knowing we fought back with everything we had. No regrets.

Except for Doctor Werner. Gods, just the thought of

him outliving me made my stomach burn. Every time I managed to make peace with myself, the doctor was always popping up in my mind to churn up a sea of bile.

This time it was Jard who spotted them first. "I see the ships," he said.

A flickering light shone like a distant candleflame. "Nigel," I said, "it's time to get loud."

"Bloody right," he replied.

Again, the ships looked like they were going to ram right into us. Choosing to trust Masato's calculations, I stayed where I was and watched them approach. They were close enough now that I could see eight separate ships with bright blinking lights.

Our jetpacks engaged for just a second but our circle of locked arms held tight. "That was just a nudge," said Masato. "We're in perfect position now."

The ships roared straight at us, though their roar was inaudible in the silence of space. I looked at Nigel, saw what little I could of his face behind his faceplate. He winked at me, and a surge of confidence burst from deep inside me.

The ships raced past, the heat of their engines warming my face.

"They heard us," said Nigel.

"How do you know?"

"Because we heard them."

"What did they say?"

"I don't know. But I could feel their curiosity."

"We did it?" I asked.

"We sure did," he said. "It's over. It's all over."

"Radio communication just opened back up," said Ghost.

"See if they don't mind coming back to pick us up," said Nigel.

For the first time since I discovered the alien threat, I felt truly weightless. Like this was the first time I ever floated in zero-g. I let go of my neighbors and let every single muscle in my body unwind as if I'd just relaxed into a hot tub.

"They can take their time," I said.

EPILOGUE

I TOOK A SEAT IN THE GRASS AND LET THE SUN warm me through the back of my coat. The ground under the patchy carpet of green was harder and rockier than it looked, so I shifted my weight until I found a comfortable position before rubbing my knee. After all these years, it still got awfully sore when I was out in the cold.

Feeling short of breath, I reached for the tank strapped over my shoulder and turned up the oxygen. I breathed deep through my nose to take advantage of the increased air supply flowing from the plastic tube under my nostrils. It was a miracle to be outside on Mars without a spacesuit, but breathing could be a challenge, especially for the elderly. Like me.

Families crowded around the monument, thirteen monoliths carved from polished red rock, one for each of the botsies who saved Mars. Children carried colorful streamers in and out between the stones, creating a tangled weave of paper and flimsy cloth that was meant to represent the many pathways of their hive communication system. Sandstorms still sometimes ripped through this area to scour the monument free of its decorations only to be adorned again after the storms cleared.

A group of children played near the fountain of carved stone and yellow water. Yellow because it was laced with antifreeze so it could operate year-round. A botsie went to the Wall of Heroes and tied a ribbon to the steel grating. I'd done the same thing ten minutes ago over the plaque that honored Navya. Just like I had on this date every year for the last forty-three years.

Masato had a plaque of his own, hung shortly after he passed. Amazingly, he'd kept that positive spirit right to the end despite a pair of failed marriages and a grueling fight against cancer. We remained close friends until the day he died. But even after he took his last breath, it was like he hadn't really left us. His daughter, Mirai Navya Moon, was the first human born with memories inherited from an AI. Mirai was her own person, but Masato was there, too. I always thought of Smith as family, but it became a fact with his daughter.

The botsie I'd been watching was tying another ribbon now, this one over Jard's plaque. He'd died just two years ago, fittingly in his workshop, where he never stopped building botsies.

Bare spaces on the wall would one day be filled with plaques honoring Nigel, Ghost, and me, the only contributors on our mission to save Mars who were still alive. The sun dipped under the horizon, and I instantly felt the chill of its absence on my back. I pulled my feet under me and with the push of two hands, lifted myself upright. After a short walk to the elevators, I descended into Red Tunnel and dropped off my oxygen tank at the rental booth.

The tunnel had changed a lot over the decades. To be sure, it still maintained some of its seedy veneer of quick-jab dealers and pharmapits, but it also had grocery stores and real estate offices as well as quite a few importers who sold a wide range of exotic spices and delicacies from around the galaxy. I headed for the ice cream shop.

My AI's voice came into my mind. <You have a call.>

With this AI, I'd had the good sense to leave her be. No injected memories or personality imprints. <Who is it?>

<Ambassador Orion.>

<Put her through, Mags.>

"Denver?"

"I'm here, Nigel. What's up?"

"It's Doctor Werner. Alvearu intelligence believes he just arrived on Mars."

I stopped in my tracks. "Werner's here?"

"They think so, but this isn't the first time they've claimed to know where he is only to see him slip away. Do you think the nanobots still work?"

"We're about to find out."

We'd claimed the nanobots would poison him if he disobeyed us back on the alien outpost decades ago. That, of course, was a ruse. Unfortunately, we didn't have the equipment or expertise to make such a change to the nanobots we'd retrieved from Ojiisan and injected into the doctor. But we did enable their tracking capability, and the little blip projected on the map inside my mind led to an old mine, where I once had a run-in with Rafe Ranchard more than half a lifetime ago.

Rafe was a nasty piece of work, emphasis on the word *was*. I counted him as an enemy vanquished just like all the others I'd gone against. Except for Doctor Werner. He was my only loss in an otherwise undefeated record. But even at my advanced age, it wasn't too late. He was here. On Mars. There could only be one reason why.

The mine wasn't active anymore. Its upper levs had been converted into condos. Down deep, it was still a warren of rough-carved tunnels and shafts. The doctor was down here, where there was nothing but rubble and broken mining equipment.

It didn't take long to find him. As always, if you wanted to find Doctor Werner, just follow the trail of bodies. I'd counted six so far. By the looks of it, they all killed themselves. Slashed wrists. Pulseripper to the head. One appeared to have propped up a large rock with a shovel before placing his head underneath it and kicking the shovel free.

How he'd lured them down here, I had no idea, but Doctor Werner looked exactly the same as I remembered. Though he'd probably shapeshifted hundreds of times over the last forty-three years to avoid capture, he was in his human form now. Oily, disheveled hair. A superior sneer that didn't have an off switch.

His beady eyes went wide with recognition, and then a broad smile broke out on his face. A device sat on an overturned ore cart. It didn't look like much, just a silver box with a few exposed wires. He pointed at the box, his face full of mirth.

Like I said, there could be only one reason he came back to Mars. He'd finally created a device that could control the human mind without driving people into the throes of red fever. Finally, a system that didn't require surgical implants. He'd always maintained it was possible, and here he was, decades later, proving he was right all along. Though the Alvearu had no need for human mind control anymore, maybe, just maybe, he could get his rights reinstated. After all, he got in trouble by defying orders to quit trying when the rest of his kind had given up the task as impossible.

It hurt to know he'd succeeded by making people kill themselves. I'd taken a lot of pride in thinking humans were impervious to mind control. In thinking we were special. But I supposed we'd earned plenty of special status by surviving the loss of our home world and the sustained attacks of the Alvearu with the help of the botsies we'd birthed into existence. Nobody else in the known history of the galaxy had done any such thing.

The doctor aimed his eyes at the floor, where a woman lay next to the ore cart. I hadn't noticed her before. Her head was blown apart, and now it was time to do the same to me.

"So good to see you, Denver." He put a finger to his lips, a pantomimed order for me to stay quiet. "You're in my control now. You couldn't speak now if you tried to," he said. "Go ahead, try. I want to hear that whiny, pathetic voice of yours. You can't, can you? I've done it, you see. The mind control system I've always promised is a reality, and thanks to your propensity to barge in where you're not invited, you've foolishly stepped in range of the device. All of these years, I was right, and you were wrong, and now the last lesson you'll learn before you die is just how insignificant and powerless you are."

He lifted his thumb and extended a finger to make his hand look like a gun. "Like the other lab rats, you'll do as ordered by my gestures." Slowly, he lifted that hand until his index finger was pressed against his temple.

I watched a pulseripper rise from its holster into my sightline. Having no control whatsoever, I cringed as the barrel turned in an unsettling direction.

The doctor waved goodbye with his other hand then flicked the thumb of his mock gun to mimic the drop of the hammer.

The gun fired, a pulse rippling out from its power source. The mind control device blew apart and scattered shrapnel against the rock wall. The doctor gasped.

I disconnected from Ghost's eyes and reacquainted myself with the elevator shaft I'd been hiding inside. Now it was me who was grinning. As we'd predicted, the mind control device had zero effect on Ghost, and now the device had been successfully destroyed.

<Ready, Mags?> I asked as I pulled the Magnum .357 from my hip holster.

<As I'll ever be,> replied the faithful AI.

I strode as fast as my old legs would take me and entered the space where Ghost held the doctor at gunpoint. The room smelled of burnt plastic and death.

"Gods, I can't stand looking at myself, Ghost. Can you shift back?"

"Of course, dear," he said. Within seconds he morphed back to his usual self. Long gray hair. Deep weathered lines around his eyes. Though he didn't have to, he was sensitive enough to age his appearance along with mine as I neared the twilight of my years.

The doctor's shoulders slumped. "You finally got me."

"Yes," I said. I didn't wait for him to say anything else. I wouldn't let him snake his way out of it this time. This time, he was going to pay for his crimes. He was going to pay for the many thousands of violent deaths caused by red fever. For the atrocities he committed on Earth. For the people he killed today.

Most of all, he was going to pay for Navya.

I squeezed the trigger.

ABOUT THE AUTHORS

WARREN HAMMOND is known for his gritty, futuristic KOP series. By taking the best of classic detective noir, and reinventing it on a destitute colony world, Hammond has created these uniquely dark tales of murder, corruption, and redemption. *KOP Killer* won the 2012 Colorado Book Award for best mystery. His last novel, *Tides of Maritinia*, was released in December of 2014. His first book independent of the KOP series, *Tides* is a spy novel set in a science fictional world.

JOSHUA VIOLA is a 2021 Splatterpunk Award nominee, five-time Colorado Book Award finalist, and editor of the *StokerCon*™ 2021 Souvenir Anthology (Horror Writers Association). He is the co-author of the Denver Moon series (Hex Publishers) with Warren Hammond. Their graphic novel, *Denver Moon: Metamorphosis*, was included on the 2018 Bram Stoker Award™ Preliminary Ballot. Viola edited the *Denver Post* bestselling horror anthology *Nightmares Unhinged* (Hex Publishers), and co-edited *Cyber World* (Hex Publishers)—named one of the best science fiction anthologies of 2016 by Barnes & Noble. His short fiction has appeared in numerous anthologies, including *One of Us: A Tribute to Frank Michaels Errington* (Bloodshot Books), *DOA III: Extreme Horror Anthology* (Blood Bound Books), *Doorbells at Dusk* (Corpus Press), and *Classic Monsters Unleashed* (Crystal Lake Publishing/Black Spot Books). He is also a regular contributor to Denver's popular art and culture magazine, *Birdy*, and has reprints available on *Tor.com*. He is the owner and chief editor of Hex Publishers in Denver, Colorado, where he lives with his husband, Aaron Lovett, their son, Orion, and their dogs, Ripley and Atari. You can learn more about Joshua Viola online at *joshuaviola.com*.

ABOUT THE ARTIST

AARON LOVETT is a mixed-heritage Asian American artist and has been published by AfterShock Comics, *Tor.com*, *The Denver Post*, and *Spectrum Fantastic Art 22 & 24*. His *Nightmares Unhinged* (Hex Publishers) cover art was licensed by AMC for their hit TV show *Fear the Walking Dead*. He was the artist for the HWA's *StokerCon™ 2021 Souvenir Anthology*. You can see his most recent work in *Monster Train* (Shiny Shoe and Good Shepherd Entertainment), which was a number one Global Top Seller on Steam and named Best Card Game of 2020 by *PC Gamer*. His art can be found in various other video games, books and comics. You can view his portfolio at *artstation.com/adlovett*. He paints from a dark corner in Denver, Colorado.

OTHER TITLES IN THE DENVER MOON SERIES

CPSIA information can be obtained
at www.ICGtesting.com
Printed in the USA
LVHW052341200922
728862LV00004B/122